Starring Meg

Praise for *Star Club*

'———— full of fun literary and movie references and ———— ———— ed with family secrets and friendship ————, this smart, charming book is perfect for ———— ———— in or Cathy Cassidy fans. I loved it!'

When Natasha was young her absolute favourite thing was reading everything she could get her hands on. Her second favourite thing was persuading her sister, brothers and neighbours to sing, dance and act with her in different shows that they performed for their parents and anyone else who would watch. Natasha loved her speech and drama classes (way more than school) and studied it right up to diploma level, taking part in various musicals and pantomimes along the way. One of her favourite books was *Ballet Shoes* by Noel Streatfeild, and she has read it so many times her copy is almost falling apart. As Natasha's siblings are now too old to be made take part in performances, she decided to create Star Club instead, and she is really enjoying writing about the kind of club she would have loved to join herself. The first book in the *Star Club* series, *Hannah in the Spotlight*, is also published by The O'Brien Press.

Also by this author, *Missing Ellen*.

Natasha Mac a'Bháird

Starring Meg

STAR
CLUB

THE O'BRIEN PRESS
DUBLIN

First published 2017 by
The O'Brien Press Ltd,
12 Terenure Road East, Rathgar,
Dublin 6, D06 HD27 Ireland.
Tel: +353 1 4923333; Fax: +353 1 4922777

E-mail: books@obrien.ie.

Website: www.obrien.ie

ISBN: 978-1-84717-846-6

7 6 5 4 3 2 1

21 20 19 18 17

Printed and bound by CPI Group (UK) Ltd, Croydon, CR0 4YY

The paper in this book is produced using pulp from managed forests.

Published in
DUBLIN
UNESCO
City of Literature

Dedication

To my sister Áine, for all the years of plays and dressing up.

Acknowledgements

Thanks so much to all the young readers who were kind enough to tell me how much they enjoyed *Hannah in the Spotlight* – you have no idea how much this means to me. I hope you will enjoy Meg's story just as much! Thank you to everyone in The O'Brien Press, especially my brilliant editor Helen Carr. And thanks as always to Aidan, Rachel and Sarah.

Chapter One

I checked my new schoolbag for probably the tenth time. Tomorrow was my first day at my new school, and I was feeling pretty nervous. Mum and I had gone shopping for all the books on the list the school had sent, and they were waiting in my bag, looking shiny and new in their plastic covers. I had a new pencil case too, shaped like a Converse boot with a zip at the top where your foot should go in. I remembered how, when I was younger, I loved the start of the school year, with all my new colouring pencils and notebooks and workbooks waiting to be filled in, all pristine and white. It was a long time since I had been to school – and even longer since I'd been to school in Ireland – so I felt almost like I had when I started off as a five-year-old, excited and anxious and not knowing what to expect.

Upstairs, Mum was in the middle of a cleaning frenzy. She'd put on some nineties music that she said made her feel young and energetic again and was singing along at the top of her voice. The music was so loud that I didn't hear the doorbell ringing. I only realised Sadie was there when she tapped on the sitting room window. I ran to open the door.

'Sorry, Sadie. Have you been waiting long?' I asked, as she came into the front hall, grimacing at the blaring music coming down the stairs.

'About five minutes,' Sadie told me, pushing her sunglasses back on top of her head with one hand – in the other one she was balancing a casserole dish and a bag of groceries. 'What's all that racket?'

Not waiting for an answer, she strode into the kitchen and set the casserole dish down on the counter. Sadie is convinced Mum doesn't feed me properly. She hadn't seen the transformation in Mum this week, though.

Sadie is my grandmother, though she looks nothing like the type of granny you might imagine, with curly grey hair and sensible shoes. She's always dressed in the latest fashions and looks very glamorous, which I suppose is fitting for an actress. She has let her hair go grey, but has it cut in a short choppy style that really suits her.

She turned to me now, asking, 'Where's your mum? I'm guessing she's out if she hasn't made you switch off that dreadful noise!'

I smiled. 'That's Mum's music actually! She's gone a bit mad these last few days, if you must know.'

'Oh?' Sadie's eyebrows went up until they disappeared under her beautifully cut fringe.

'Come and see for yourself,' I told her.

I led the way upstairs, just as Mum began screeching along to 'Brimful of Asha'. Mum was kneeling on the bathroom floor wearing old jeans and bright yellow rubber gloves and scrubbing the tiles so hard it looked like she was trying to take the surface off them.

'Good heavens!' said Sadie.

Mum jumped – the music was so loud she hadn't heard us coming. Cornershop – Mum's favourite band – were blaring out that 'everybody needs a bosom for a pillow'. Sadie reached over and switched the music off.

'Who are you and what have you done with my daughter?' Sadie wanted to know. 'I didn't realise you owned a pair of rubber gloves, Cordelia.'

Mum got to her feet, using the bit of her arm not covered in rubber glove to push a strand of hair out of her face. 'Oh, hello, Sadie, I didn't hear you come in.'

'What's going on here?' Sadie asked, looking around the room almost as if she'd discovered Mum having a wild party instead of cleaning the bathroom. 'The last time I remember you being this houseproud was when you were expecting Meg and the nesting instinct kicked in!'

Mum laughed. 'Well, that's definitely not the case this time. I just want everything perfect for Meg starting school.'

'I don't think my teacher is going to ask to come over and check behind the toilet, Mum,' I told her.

'How about a nice cup of tea?' Sadie suggested. 'You look like you could do with a break.'

Mum surveyed the bathroom. Everything was gleaming and even the shampoo bottles were arranged in neat rows like soldiers.

'Good idea,' she said. 'Stick the kettle on, Meg darling. I'll be down in two shakes of a lamb's tail, just after I scrub around the taps with an old toothbrush.'

The thing about Mum is, whenever she gets a new idea into her head she just throws herself into it heart and soul. Like the time she did an evening class in pottery. She embraced the whole pottery thing with this wild enthusiasm, making one bowl after another, then (because they were easy) dozens of ashtrays, even though no one in the family smokes. She moved on to jugs next, which were a lot trickier, especially the handles, which she never quite managed to work out. This didn't faze Mum one bit – she just turned the wonky-handled jugs into vases and spent hours painting and decorating them. When she ran out of places to display them she started giving them away to anyone who came to the house.

Then just as suddenly as she'd started, Mum got tired of the whole thing, bundled the vases and ashtrays and bowls into a box and brought them all to the charity shop, and took up tennis instead. Last time I was looking for something in Sadie's garage I found Mum's old potter's wheel, which she'd splashed out on at the height of her pottery craze and then forgotten all about.

Now, it seemed, Mum had decided that Being an Ordinary Mum was her new thing. Only Mum doesn't do ordinary, so she was in fact taking it to extraordinary lengths.

We'd moved to Carrickbeg, where Mum grew up and where Sadie and Grandad still live, at the start of the summer. Mum had got a new job almost straight away, and she'd been really busy. Then she'd had a sudden attack of the guilts that the summer was nearly over and she hadn't done any mother-daughter stuff with me. And the fact that Dad was working abroad and only came home for occasional visits seemed to make her feel she had to make it up to me by being twice as much fun. She persuaded her boss to give her the week off – Mum can be very persuasive. We'd gone on all sorts of day trips, to the beach, the museum, the cinema, and even on a bus tour of Dublin city. And of course there were the essential shopping trips too, where Mum bought a ton of new clothes for both of us (even though I have to wear a horrible grey uniform to my new school).

We'd had a fabulous week, but I was exhausted by the end of it and was kind of relieved when Mum said we'd stay at home for the weekend so she could get things ready for us going back to school and work. I didn't realise what she had in mind, which turned out to be a total spring clean of the entire house.

I put on the kettle, while Sadie unpacked the groceries and started putting things away in the fridge.

'I'm starting to wonder if I've come to the right house at all,' she commented, looking into the sparkling clean fridge, which was full of fruit and vegetables and natural yogurt. Mum had even made a quinoa salad with chopped peppers and cucumber and divided it into individual portions for our packed lunches. 'How long has this been going on?'

'You know Mum,' I told her. 'When she decides she's into something, nothing's going to stop her. It just so happens that this week she's into being some kind of super mum.'

'Well, if this is the result I'm in favour of it,' Sadie observed. 'It's certainly better than that eco-living phase when she stopped washing her hair.'

Mum came in, peeling off her rubber gloves, which she at once folded and put away with the cleaning things. 'Oh Sadie, did you bring groceries? You shouldn't have.'

'I thought you might need a few things for school lunches and so on,' Sadie said. 'But I can see you have it all under control.'

'Of course,' Mum said. 'Everything's going to be perfect

for my little girl's big day. It's *such* an important milestone in her life.'

She kissed the top of my head. I made a face at Sadie, who tried to hide her smile.

The truth was that the more Mum went on about what a big deal school was, the more nervous I felt. I hadn't been to school in over a year. I'd had lessons, of course, with different teachers, and I'd studied on my own too, but when you're moving around all the time normal school isn't really an option. And Mum said there was no way she was sending me to boarding school because she'd miss me too much.

At first, not going to school was a kind of adventure, and I loved spending more time with my parents and not having a rigid schedule. I didn't even mind having to do lessons on my own, because I could work at my own pace, and I usually managed to wangle things so that we spent lots of time on the things I loved, like English and art, and as little time as possible on maths and geography.

But the longer I spent out of school, the more I started to miss being with kids my own age. And at the same time it became harder and harder to imagine going to a new school and having to start all over again. The thought of it built up in my head, getting scarier all the time. Now, when I knew I was facing it the very next day, it was frankly terrifying.

Sadie seemed to see how I was feeling better than Mum did. 'Oh, there's no need for such a drama, Cordelia,' she said lightly. 'It's a perfectly ordinary thing to start a new school. People do it all the time. And it's not like Meg won't know anyone. She has her lovely new friends from Star Club, don't you, darling?'

'Yes, they're all in my class,' I said, grateful to Sadie for looking on the bright side as always. I knew I was incredibly lucky to have Hannah, Ruby and Laura there for support. I'd only known them since the start of the summer, but we'd become very close, and I felt sure they'd look out for me in school. Just knowing I'd have somebody to talk to in the yard at break time made me feel better.

'There you go then! How many children have to start school not knowing anyone? Or even not knowing the language? Like little Mariola who lives near me – her parents are both Polish, and she barely had a word of English starting school! But she soon settled in – Carrickbeg National School is always so welcoming to new children. Meg will be just fine.'

'Oh, of course she will,' Mum said. 'But that doesn't mean I can't make a fuss of my precious girl on her big day, does it?'

I cast a desperate look at Sadie, who rose to the occasion brilliantly. 'Meg, speaking of your friends, I think I saw some of them out on the green when I was coming in earlier. Why don't you go out for a while? I'm sure you need to make plans for tomorrow.'

She took the teapot from me and went to the kettle. 'I'll look after the tea. Off you go now.'

'Thanks, Sadie,' I said, glad to escape.

'Don't go too far!' Mum said. 'It's nearly bedtime and we'd better make it an early night.'

'OK, Mum,' I called back, already halfway out the door.

Chapter Two

Outside, I realised that Sadie hadn't just been making something up to let me escape. Hannah and Laura were sitting on the wall between Hannah's house and mine. Hannah's long, light-brown hair hung down loose, almost touching the wall where she was sitting, while Laura's dark curly hair was drawn back in a ponytail. As I went to join them the door opened at Ruby's house on the other side of the green and she ran over to join us. She had put on a pink wraparound cardigan over the leotard and leggings she wears to do her ballet exercises, which she's really disciplined about.

'Mum said I can have five minutes before bedtime,' Ruby said, hopping up on the wall beside Laura.

'Me too, pretty much,' I said, taking my place beside Hannah.

'Can you believe we're back to early bedtimes and all that stuff?' Hannah said with a sigh. 'I don't know where the summer holidays went – the last few weeks just seemed to disappear.'

'It's always like that,' Laura said. 'At the start of the holidays you feel like you have masses of time to do everything you want, then when it comes to the last few weeks time seems to speed up and you realise you didn't do half the things you had planned.'

'We didn't even get started on another show for Star Club,' Hannah said sadly.

After Mum and I moved in next door to the Kielys at the start of the summer, Hannah and I made friends right away, and when we realised we both loved acting it was the start of Hannah's great idea to set up Star Club. Star Club is me, Hannah, Ruby and Laura. Ruby loves ballet and is an amazing dancer, and Laura writes stories (though I haven't actually seen any of them yet – she's kind of secretive about them).

We're only twelve, but we are trying to make our theatre group as professional as we can. It had been so much fun working on something as a group and using all our different types of creativity to put a performance together. I'd found it so different from the types of acting I'd done before, where I'd have to do a scene over and over again until it was right, and where I was often the only child on set. I loved any kind of acting – but the kind where I also got to hang out with my new friends was hard to beat.

A few weeks earlier we put on our first show, which took place in Hannah's garden. It was for her little sister Maisie's birthday party, and lots of the neighbours came as well as Maisie's friends. We loved the whole experience and were planning to do another show – but with one thing and another we hadn't managed to get started yet.

'I thought we might start something when I got back from Spain, but then Laura was away,' Ruby said.

'I was going to suggest having a meeting this week, but Mum wanted to pack a whole summer's worth of outings into one week!' I said. The girls had heard all about my crazy week already.

'At least you got to do fun stuff,' Hannah said. '*My* week seemed to mainly consist of shopping for uniforms and helping Mum find everyone's lunch boxes, which they'd managed to lose over the holidays. Bobby's still had a banana in it. At least it used to be a banana.'

'Ewwww!' exclaimed Ruby.

'I know!'

'Well, let's try to meet up some day after school,' Laura said. 'Maybe once we're back in a regular routine we'll find it easier to plan our club meetings.'

Hannah's face lit up at once. She just loves organising things. 'Yes, we should start planning! What days are we going to have our meetings? We said we'd have regular days once school started.'

'I've got ballet on Tuesdays, Thursdays and Saturday mornings,' Ruby said. 'So they're out for me.'

'And you and I have Gaelic football on Wednesday,' Laura reminded Hannah.

I didn't say anything. I didn't have any activities lined up yet, and didn't know if I would. Getting used to a new school might be enough for now.

'Monday and Friday then?' Hannah suggested. 'That could work well – we could do our planning on Mondays and then on Fridays when we have no homework we'd have more time to rehearse.'

'Sounds good to me,' I said, and Laura and Ruby nodded too.

'Hannah!' It was Hannah's dad at the door. 'Time to come in.'

Hannah sighed. 'I guess someone had to be first.' She scrambled down from the wall. 'See you tomorrow, OK?'

A wave of panic swept over me all of a sudden at the thought of the next morning and going in to my new school for the first time. 'You *will* still call for me on the way to school, won't you?' I said.

'Of course I will,' Hannah said reassuringly. 'I'll call at 8.15 and we can walk down together.'

My new school, the one the other three girls had been going to for seven years now, was about a ten-minute walk away. Mum had said she would drive me there and bring me in, but I'd absolutely refused to let her. Hannah said everyone from Woodland Green walked to school, with their parents if they were in the younger classes, but definitely with their friends once they reached sixth class. I didn't want to be the odd one out. Plus the thought of Mum getting all weepy and emotional at leaving me was enough to fill anyone with horror. After the way she'd been acting lately I could just imagine her behaving like the mum of a five-year-old starting school for the first time. It seemed to me that scenes like that were best played out in the privacy of our own home. The last thing I wanted was to start school with people already thinking I came from some sort of crazy family.

'Should we call for you too, Ruby?' I asked as Hannah headed inside.

Ruby shook her head. 'I wish I could walk down with you guys, but Mum got the dates mixed up and thought we weren't back to school until Wednesday. She made a dentist appointment for me first thing tomorrow morning, so I'm going to be late getting to school. I'll be there by break time though so we can catch up then.'

'I notice no one's offering to call for me,' Laura said with a grin.

'Sorry, Laura,' I said. Laura's the only one of us who doesn't live in Woodland Green. I felt bad for her that she'd be walking to school on her own. I was so glad I'd have Hannah with me.

'That's OK,' Laura said. 'I get more time for daydreaming when I'm on my own!'

Ruby's mum was the next one to appear at the door and call her in.

'I'd better go too, I suppose,' Laura said. She grabbed her bike, which was propped up against the wall, and got ready to go.

'Oh well, if you're all abandoning me,' I said with a laugh. I was often the last one to be called in, I'd noticed. I wondered if it was because I was an only child that Mum treated me as a bit more grown up, or maybe just that we'd had such a different lifestyle, free from set routines.

We all called our goodbyes as we headed off in separate directions.

When I got inside Mum was ironing my new school uniform while Sadie finished her cup of tea.

I eyed the uniform in disgust. 'Ugh, I can't believe I have to wear that thing.' Last time I'd been to school, it was an elementary school in New York, when Mum was in a play in Broadway that ran for over a year. Only the posh private schools in New York had uniforms, and my school was definitely not one of those. I much preferred being able to wear my own clothes – T-shirts and shorts in summer, warm skirts, jeans and jumpers in winter and fur-lined boots for walking to school along snowy city footpaths.

'I know, darling, it's simply awful, isn't it?' Mum said, holding the green pleated skirt up. The grey shirt and jumper were already hanging up, with the grey and green striped tie draped over the jumper's hanger. 'At least you get to wear your own jacket. When I was in school we had a dreadful blazer to match as well. Too bulky and absolutely no use at keeping you dry!'

Mum went to Carrickbeg National School too, so at least she can sympathise.

'I remember,' Sadie said with a shudder. 'You hated that blazer. In fact I seem to remember it going missing on a few occasions.'

'I can't think what you mean, Sadie,' Mum said innocently, winking at me.

I rubbed the material of the skirt between my fingers. 'Why do they have to make it so scratchy?'

'At least you'll blend in, darling,' Mum said.

It's kind of hard to get used to Mum wanting me to blend in, when for the first twelve years of my life she and Dad were always trying to get me to stand out.

'I'd better let you get to bed,' Sadie said, putting her empty mug down beside the sink. 'Have a great day tomorrow, Meg – I'm looking forward to hearing all about it.'

Sadie blew a kiss to Mum. I went to the door to wave her off, and she leaned in to give me a hug, pressing something into my hand. It was a gold locket in the shape of a heart.

'This is my lucky locket,' she told me. 'Take it with you tomorrow. You can keep it in your pocket or tuck it inside your school shirt. It's always brought me luck when I've been worried about a performance. Now don't worry about a thing, you'll be absolutely fine.'

She kissed me and dashed off. I opened the locket. Inside, instead of a photo, there was a pressed flower petal. I smiled, remembering now that Sadie had shown me this locket years earlier. The petal came from the bunch of roses Grandad had given Sadie after her very first play, when he was trying to convince her to go on a date with him. The petal was dry and paper thin, but still a beautiful soft pink. I shut the locket carefully and closed my fingers around it, feeling the comforting weight in my hand.

Back in the kitchen Mum was folding up the ironing board.

'I think I'll get some toast and hot milk,' I said. 'Maybe it will help me sleep.'

'I'll get it,' Mum said. 'You bring that ghastly uniform upstairs and get into your pyjamas, and I'll have a nice supper waiting for you when you come back down.'

When I came down a few minutes later Mum had made me a big mug of hot chocolate and a plate of toast with strawberry jam. The hot chocolate was made with foamed milk and looked delicious. Mum's not the most domesticated person and normally can't even make hot milk without it boiling over, so I appreciated the gesture. She'd even found some marshmallows, which she'd arranged in a semicircle on the saucer.

'Thanks, Mum,' I said. 'This is great.'

Mum looked pleased with herself. 'I know you're feeling nervous about your big day, so I wanted to be extra nice to you, darling!'

'I am a bit nervous,' I admitted. 'It's pretty nerve-wracking starting at a new school in sixth class. Everyone else is going to have known each other since they were four or five.'

'Oh, that reminds me!' Mum exclaimed. 'The woman next door called in earlier. She said they'd been away visiting relatives for August so she hadn't called in before. Funny sort of woman. She kept staring at my hair as if there was something extraordinary about it.'

I tried not to smile. Mum generally looks quite glamorous (for a mother) but today she'd tied a headscarf round her head to protect it from all the dust in her cleaning frenzy. She probably thought she looked sophisticated in a fifties movie star sort of way, but since the headscarf was actually a sarong I'd had on holidays, with ice cream cones and lovehearts printed all over it, she did look a tiny bit odd.

'She has a daughter in your class – Tracey, I think she said,' Mum went on. 'She's been away staying with her aunt since they came home from their holidays, otherwise I'm sure you would have bumped into her. But she's home now and her mum said she could walk to school with you tomorrow and show you the way. I told her that would be wonderful, since you've absolutely refused to let your old mum go with you!'

'Oh, but I've said I'll walk with Hannah,' I said.

Mum dismissed this with a wave of her hand. 'You can all go together, can't you? Nice for you to make more friends. There are other things in life besides Star Club, you know!'

I tried to picture the girl next door as I sipped my hot chocolate. I thought I remembered seeing her just after we'd moved in, but I didn't remember Hannah saying anything about her. Though maybe if she'd been away most of the holidays that was why.

'Goodness, look at the time!' Mum exclaimed. 'You'd better get off to bed, Meg. Early start tomorrow.'

'Don't remind me,' I said. 'I think the whole getting up early thing might actually be worse than the uniform.'

'Now don't exaggerate, honey,' Mum said. 'Nothing could be worse than that thing!' She shuddered again. 'I think we should go shopping at the weekend and buy you some nice hair things so at least you have something to brighten it up a bit! Now off you go.'

I kissed Mum goodnight and headed upstairs, still feeling a bit nervous about what the new day would bring.

Chapter Three

I was standing in the centre of the stage wearing a long emerald green gown with a sweeping train. A diamond-studded tiara sparkled on my hair, which was swept up on top of my head in an elegant chignon. The audience were roaring my name as my fellow actors clapped and I took one bow after another.

Then a deafening ringing sound interrupted the applause. At first I wondered if the theatre was on fire, but through a sleepy fog I realised it was my alarm clock. The stage faded away as I reached out to switch it off and struggled to open my eyes to the familiar sight of my bedroom. I was at home in Carrickbeg, and I had to get up for school.

I groaned and pulled my duvet over my head. After a summer of lie-ins, being woken by that horrible noise felt cruel.

Mum appeared at my bedroom door, already dressed in

one of the smart suits she'd bought when she started her new job in an office. 'Oh, good, you're awake, I was just coming to call you.'

I peered at my alarm clock, trying to make my eyes open properly. 'Is it really 7.30? It feels like the middle of the night.'

Mum laughed. 'I'm afraid so, darling. The sun is shining and the birds are singing! Come on, up you get. Breakfast in fifteen minutes.'

I stumbled out of bed, grimacing once more when I saw my new uniform hanging on the wardrobe door. Horrible scratchy thing. That was one thing I was convinced I'd never get used to.

Delicious smells started wafting upstairs as I got dressed. What was Mum doing? This domestic goddess thing was so unlike her, but I certainly wasn't going to complain.

'Ta – da!' Mum said as I came into the kitchen, holding out a plate of pancakes with a flourish. 'Pancakes for my special girl on her special day!'

'Did you really make these?' I asked, looking in awe at the pile of golden fluffy pancakes topped with blueberries and maple syrup.

Mum looked delighted with herself. 'I really did. I just googled simple pancake recipes and it turned out to be far easier than I thought! Aren't they fabulous? Quick, come and eat them before they go cold.'

The pancakes were as delicious as they looked. 'Watch out, Mum,' I joked as I finished the last one. 'I'm going to be expecting this every morning now.'

Mum laughed. 'Sorry, darling, but I can't see that happening, can you? I've had to get up ten minutes earlier as it is, and you know how I like my beauty sleep.'

She drained the last of her coffee. 'Is that the time? I'd better get going. Can't be late on my first day back. Now, are you sure you don't want me to give you a lift to school?'

'Positive,' I said firmly. 'I'll walk with Hannah – and Tracey too, I suppose.'

'All right then – but I bet you'll be glad of a lift another day when it's lashing rain!'

Mum put her phone in her handbag and found her keys. Then she grabbed me in a tight hug and kissed me on both cheeks before dashing off to work.

I put the breakfast dishes in the dishwasher, brushed my teeth and checked my new schoolbag once again to make sure I had everything in it. I took out the Irish book to have a look at it again – it was a long time since I'd done Irish, I hoped it wasn't going to be too hard to keep up with the rest of the class.

I was ready to go by 8.10, but 8.15 came and went and there was no sign of Hannah. I locked the front door and went out to the garden, leaning against the wall between our two houses as I waited for her to show up.

I checked my watch again – it was 8.20 now. If we didn't leave soon we'd be late, and I wasn't exactly keen on getting into trouble on my first day. I decided I'd better pop over to Hannah's and see what was keeping her.

As I reached the doorstep I could hear the sound of complete bedlam inside – but that's not unusual for Hannah's family. Hannah is the oldest of five, and her brothers Zach and Bobby and her sister Maisie would be getting ready for school too, while baby Emma would probably be mad at being left out. I rang the doorbell, wondering if it would be heard over all the noise.

There was the usual scuffle that always seems to follow the doorbell ringing in the Kiely house and I heard shouts of 'I'll get it' and 'No, I said I was getting it!' from different kids. Eventually Bobby, who's the middle child in the family and seems to be extra noisy to make up for it, opened the door. He was still in his pyjamas and was eating a piece of toast. Maisie, who's six, squeezed her head around Bobby to see who it was.

'Hi guys,' I said. 'Is Hannah ready?'

'I doubt it,' Maisie said. 'We slept in.' She looked pretty happy about this, I thought.

Hannah came running down the stairs, also still in her pyjamas. My heart sank – just how late were we going to be?

'Meg, I'm so sorry,' she said. 'We all slept in – Dad was

supposed to call us, but *someone* was playing with his phone yesterday and switched off the alarm.' She cast a cross look at Bobby, who looked as unconcerned as Maisie and went on munching on his toast.

'How long do you think you'll be?' I asked, trying not to sound as worried as I felt.

'At least another ten minutes,' Hannah said. 'I'm really sorry. Dad said he'll drive us so we're not too late, but we don't have room in the car for you too.'

I swallowed a lump in my throat. 'No worries. I'll just head off now and I'll see you there.'

'I'm so sorry,' Hannah said for the third time. 'You know where you're going, right?'

'Of course — straight down the hill — it would be hard to go wrong.' I made my voice sound as light-hearted as possible. 'I'd better go then. See you later.'

Bobby was already closing the door. I turned and walked quickly down Hannah's drive, not wanting them to see how upset I was.

'Hi, you must be Meg.' A girl with frizzy brown hair and freckles was standing on the path just outside my house. She was wearing the grey Carrickbeg National School uniform and carrying a schoolbag covered in graffiti.

'Hi,' I said. 'Are you Tracey?'

'Yes — we can walk to school together if you like,' Tracey said. Her eyes swept up and down me as if she was examining my uniform, though it was exactly the same as her own.

'Sure,' I said. 'I was supposed to go with Hannah, but she's not ready.'

'Oh no, I hope you're not too upset,' Tracey said, her eyes widening in concern. 'It's awful when you're depending on someone and they let you down.'

'No, it's fine,' I said. 'Hannah couldn't help it – her dad's alarm didn't go off.'

'Oh, is that what she said? Wow, that's pretty careless. If I was supposed to be meeting someone on their first day at a new school I'd set my own alarm,' Tracey said. 'Still, I'm sure Hannah didn't mean to leave you stranded like that. But don't worry, I'll show you the way to go and everything.'

'Thanks,' I said. I wondered if I should stick up for Hannah, but actually I felt pretty cross that she wasn't there for me. She knew how nervous I was about starting at a new school and how much it meant to me that we would go in together. Why couldn't she have made sure she was ready on time like she promised?

I decided to change the subject. 'So how come I haven't seen you about all summer?'

'We were away for ages in America,' Tracey said. 'We were visiting my uncle in Florida, and then when we got home I went to stay with my aunt in Dublin for a few days.'

'Oh, lucky you!' I said. 'Was it really hot in Florida?'

'Boiling,' Tracey said. 'We couldn't even go outside in the middle of the day. But my uncle has a pool in his back garden so as soon as it got to about three o'clock we were out there sunbathing and jumping into the water to cool down. I so want to move there some day!'

'I miss the sun,' I said with a sigh. The Irish weather was one thing I was struggling to get used to.

'Did you used to live somewhere sunny?' Tracey asked.

'Yes, we were in the States for the last few years – California. My dad got transferred out there for work.' I didn't look at her as I spoke, not wanting her to think these were lines I'd rehearsed, even though that was exactly what they were. Mum and I had talked about it a lot and agreed that this was the best approach – not an outright lie, but definitely not telling the whole story either. People were bound to look at me differently if they knew my mum was an actress and my dad was a film director in Hollywood. It was better if they got to know me as me and not because of who my family were.

'Wow, you're the lucky one,' Tracey said. 'I'd love to live in California – it must be amazing!'

'It was great for a few years, but I was kind of glad to come home really,' I said. 'I missed Sadie and Grandad.' I told her about my grandparents, and she chatted about her family too – her mum and dad and her little brother

Tyler, who sounded pretty annoying if Tracey's descriptions were anything to go by. Most people seem to find their siblings annoying – something that's hard for me to understand as an only child.

'Have you been hanging out with Hannah and the others the whole time?' Tracey asked.

'Pretty much,' I said. 'It's been so nice to make some new friends.'

'I saw a bit of that show you did in Hannah's garden,' Tracey told me. 'You were amazing! Have you done a lot of acting?'

'Oh – a bit,' I said, blushing again. 'Do you like acting?'

'I love it,' Tracey said. 'I'd have loved to join in, but I knew Hannah wouldn't want me.'

'Why?' I asked, feeling puzzled. Hannah had been so kind to me and made me part of her gang. I couldn't imagine her leaving someone out.

'Oh, I know she doesn't mean to exclude people,' Tracey said. 'She's just so busy with all her brothers and sisters, and she and Laura and Ruby have been friends for years. I guess they don't really have room for anyone else.'

I felt a bit uneasy. Was Tracey right? Maybe I was pushing my way into a group of friends that didn't want new people. Maybe Hannah had just felt she had to look after me because I was new to the area.

'Anyway, things are always different in the summer holidays, aren't they?' Tracey went on, not seeming to notice my discomfort. 'You hang out with neighbours a lot more because you're at home and you've got loads of time. It'll all be different now that we're back at school.'

As we got closer to the school, the footpath became crowded with boys and girls wearing the same grey uniform as us – little ones being dropped off by their parents, carrying schoolbags almost as big as themselves, kids on scooters and bikes, and bigger ones our age walking along in twos and threes.

We reached the school gates, and I felt butterflies rise up in my tummy once more. This was so much worse than getting on a stage. At least then I was being someone else and had lines learned off and knew exactly what I had to do. That thought gave me an idea. I might not have my lines learned, but I could certainly pretend to be someone else – someone who was an ordinary schoolgirl who knew exactly what she was doing and wouldn't dream of being nervous about such a simple thing as walking into school. Someone who wasn't trying to hide who she really was. I slipped my hand into my pocket where I'd put Sadie's locket and ran my fingers over the intricate pattern. I held my head up high as we went into the yard.

'You're in sixth class, aren't you?' Tracey said.

I nodded. So confident, so nonchalant about the whole thing, I didn't even need to speak.

'We have to line up over here,' she told me, indicating a line in the yard where kids were already standing in little groups, chatting and laughing. The girls were greeting each other with hugs and the boys with friendly punches – that was one thing that was just the same as my old school, I thought. I spotted Laura with some other girls and was about to go and join her, but Tracey grabbed my arm.

'We'd better go in at the back here,' she said. 'The principal is really strict about the lines in the morning. You don't want to make a bad impression.'

'Oh, right, thanks,' I said, grateful to Tracey for the advice.

We joined the back of the line, behind some boys who were chatting about their summer holidays, just as the bell started ringing. As the oldest class in the school, it looked like our class had to go in first, and the kids at the top of the line started moving off. I lost sight of Laura as we trooped into the narrow school corridor.

Tracey showed me which was our classroom – a bright, airy room, looking almost painfully neat with the desks lined up in perfectly straight rows. Apart from a couple of charts the walls were completely bare after the summer holidays, though I knew in a few weeks they'd be covered in artwork and projects once more. Miss Brennan, a young, smiley woman with her hair in a ponytail, was standing near the door, greeting the kids as they came in.

Everyone was exclaiming over each other like long-lost friends, and Tracey started chatting to one of the boys. I hung back, feeling a bit left out. But Tracey soon turned back to me, smiling at me warmly.

'We can sit wherever we like for the first week,' she told me. 'Why don't we grab these two seats beside Jamie?'

She indicated the back row, where the boy she'd been talking to had just sat down. There were only two seats left. I hesitated – where were my Star Club friends going to be sitting? Shouldn't I wait for them?

I spotted Laura waving to me from the front row, and pointing to a seat beside her. I looked at Tracey, not wanting to abandon her after she'd been so nice. I saw there were a few empty seats near Laura.

'Let's go up the front near Laura,' I suggested. 'There's plenty of room for us both.'

Tracey grabbed my bag and set it down on the chair in the back row. 'No, we're fine here. I'm not sitting right in front of the teacher. You don't want people to think you're a teacher's pet, do you?'

Laura was looking at me with a funny expression on her face, still gesturing to the seat beside her. I stood there, wavering, wondering how to handle it. I thought of Hannah and how we were supposed to walk to school together. If she'd kept her promise I'd be sitting beside her now and I wouldn't have to risk offending either Laura or

Tracey. A feeling of resentment swept over me – why did Hannah have to let me down?

'All right, settle down class, take your seats!' The teacher strode to the front of the classroom. The decision was made for me – there was no way I was going to draw attention to myself now by moving up front. I hurriedly took the seat beside Tracey, trying to ignore the hurt look Laura gave me.

Just then Hannah came rushing into the room, her schoolbag flying behind her. She stopped dead when she saw me, a look of shock on her face. I took no notice, concentrating hard on taking out my pencil case and notebook and lining them up on the desk in front of me.

'Ah, Hannah, you made it,' Miss Brennan said. 'I hope this isn't a case of starting as you mean to go on?'

'No, miss, sorry – our alarm didn't go off,' Hannah murmured, sliding into the seat beside Laura as quickly as she could.

'Well, you're just in time,' Miss Brennan said. 'Now class, I'm your teacher, Miss Brennan. And I believe we have a new student joining us this year. Where is Meg Howard?'

I raised my hand, blushing red at having attention drawn to me like this. I hoped Miss Brennan wasn't going to ask me to stand up and tell the class something about myself. I would absolutely die of embarrassment.

But Miss Brennan just smiled at me and said, 'You're

very welcome, Meg. Please let me know if you need any help with anything. And that goes for the rest of you too, boys and girls! Now, I'd like to get to know you all a little better. Why don't you tell me something about what you did in your summer holidays? Who'd like to go first?'

Chapter Four

When the bell rang for break I was about to go and join Laura and Hannah, but Tracey put a hand on my arm to stop me. 'Make sure Hannah knows you're still upset that she let you down this morning,' she whispered. 'You should wait until she comes to you.'

I looked at her in surprise. 'What do you mean?'

Tracey glanced quickly at Hannah from beneath her fringe, then turned to whisper to me again, gripping my arm. 'Don't just go up to her like nothing happened or she'll think she can walk all over you.'

'It's not like that,' I said. I'd had time to get over what had happened earlier, and even though I'd been upset I knew Hannah would never have deliberately let me down. 'It's no big deal.'

Tracey seemed to change her attitude at once. Straightening up, she said quickly, 'No, you're right, better to let it go. It's always nice to be the bigger person!'

'Come on, let's go outside,' Jamie said. 'We usually play rounders at break time.'

As soon as we got out to the yard Laura and Hannah came running over to me. Tracey and Jamie went off to join another group who were picking teams for rounders.

'How come you're not sitting with us?' Laura asked. 'I saved a place for you.'

'Sorry,' I said. 'Tracey didn't want to sit up the front, and I didn't really want to leave her. She was really nice showing me the way to school.'

Laura made a kind of snorting noise. 'Tracey? She's only ever nice when she wants something.'

'What do you mean?' I asked, confused.

Laura and Hannah looked at each other, as if each of them wanted the other to say something.

'Let's not get into all that,' Hannah said quickly. 'It doesn't really matter where we sit, anyway. Miss Brennan will probably mix us all up again by the end of the week. They only usually let us sit where we like for the first few days.'

'Miss Brennan seems nice, doesn't she?' I said, relieved to change the subject. 'Have you guys had her before?'

'No, she's kind of new to the school,' Hannah said. 'I think she just started the year before last.'

'Didn't Isabel's brother's class have her last year?' Laura said.

'No, they had Mr Simms, don't you remember how Ben used to complain about him the whole time?' Hannah said.

'Oh, that's right, and we were all like, what are you complaining about? Miss Ford is so much worse,' Laura said.

'Miss Ford! She was such a nightmare!' Hannah said. 'Remember how she used to take ten minutes off Golden Time if someone got a spelling wrong? It was so unfair!'

'I know! Ten minutes for one tiny little mistake! Some weeks we didn't get any Golden Time at all! She was so mean.'

I felt kind of left out. I didn't know any of the teachers they were talking about, or Isabel or Ben either. And I didn't know what on earth Golden Time was. It was like there was this whole new world of school that I wasn't a part of, but my friends were.

Hannah and Laura were still talking about Miss Ford and how awful she was. I tried to change the subject. 'Do you think Miss Brennan will let us do drama?'

'She'll have to because it's on the curriculum,' Laura said.

'Yeah, but it does depend on the teacher how much time we get to spend on it,' Hannah pointed out. 'Remember Miss Ford hardly did any?'

'Anyway, we've got Star Club later,' I said, hoping they wouldn't start complaining about Miss Ford again. 'Are we going to start planning another show?'

'Definitely,' Hannah said. 'I can't wait to get started on something. Let's all try to have some ideas for later, OK? Oh look, here's Ruby, I'll tell her too.'

Ruby came running over to join us, her schoolbag still on her back. 'Hi guys! No fillings today, phew! I'd better put my schoolbag in the classroom.'

'Just leave it on the bench,' Laura said. 'Otherwise you're going to waste too much of break time!'

'Good idea,' Ruby said, dumping her bag on the nearest bench. 'What's going on? Are you not playing rounders today?'

'We're just talking about our Star Club meeting,' Hannah said. 'I was just saying everyone should bring some ideas to the meeting later.'

'Are we going to do something from another book?' Ruby asked. '*Ballet Shoes* was so much fun.'

For our first show, we'd picked scenes from *Ballet Shoes* by Noel Streatfeild. I hadn't read it before the other girls told me about it, but Hannah loaned it to me and I loved it right away. It's set in London in the 1930s and is about three orphan girls who have to go to stage school so they can earn their own living. I played Petrova, the middle sister, who is much more interested in cars and aeroplanes than in being on the stage. I loved playing the part – probably because Petrova is so different from me, it was quite a fun challenge bringing her to life.

'Maybe we could write something ourselves this time,' Laura said. 'I've got a few ideas we could talk about later.'

'That sounds like fun,' I said. 'It would be a good challenge to create characters from scratch.'

'What's your dad working on at the moment?' Hannah asked. 'He's gone back to Hollywood, hasn't he?'

Just as she said it Hannah turned bright red and clapped her hand over her mouth, looking at someone over my shoulder.

'Does your dad work in Hollywood?' It was Tracey, who seemed to have crept up behind us as quietly as a cat. 'What is he, some kind of an actor? Is he famous?'

I said the first thing that came into my head. 'Oh, Hannah's just joking around. You know I told you my dad worked in California for a while, so that's all she means. But nothing as glamorous as Hollywood I'm afraid.' I forced a laugh.

'Oh, that's too bad, I was hoping he might take us all to some fabulous film premiere!' Tracey laughed. 'There's the bell – we'd better line up.'

I moved quickly to the line, trying to look totally unconcerned, though my heart was pounding. I couldn't believe what had just happened. After all the times I'd stressed to my friends that I didn't want everyone knowing about my family, Hannah had gone and let the secret out on the very first day of school. I just had to hope I'd managed to convince Tracey there was nothing in it.

Hannah came running up to me as we reached the classroom door, her face still crimson. 'Meg, I'm so sorry,' she whispered. 'I had no idea Tracey was there.'

'Just be more careful, will you?' I snapped. 'You know I don't want people knowing.'

'I know. I'm really sorry. I've got such a big mouth.'

Hannah looked so guilt-stricken that I relaxed a bit. 'OK, I know you didn't mean it. Hopefully no one else heard. Tracey seems really nice, anyway. Maybe I should just tell her, since we're neighbours.'

'I don't think that's a good idea,' Hannah said quickly. 'You see …'

'All right, girls, break time's over, into your places.' Miss Brennan was already handing out worksheets. I sat down beside Tracey, who smiled warmly at me. Hannah hesitated a moment before going back to her seat beside Laura. I realised Ruby was sitting beside them too. The three of them looked so close – like they didn't need anyone else in their little group. To my horror I felt a lump rising up in my throat. I swallowed quickly and clutched Sadie's locket tightly in my hand.

'Are you stuck? Look, start with this one, it's the easiest,' Tracey whispered to me, showing me what to do on the worksheet. I smiled at her gratefully. I found myself thinking about what Laura had said about Tracey and deciding it couldn't possibly be true. Then again, it wasn't like Laura to make things up – or was it? Maybe I didn't know her – or any of them – as well as I thought.

Chapter Five

It was quite a relief when the final bell went. Hannah rushed to catch up with me as we lined up to leave the classroom. 'Let's walk home together,' she suggested.

'I can't,' I said.

'You're not still mad about earlier, are you?' Hannah asked anxiously.

'No, it's fine, but Sadie's actually picking me up,' I told her.

Mum would still be in work when school finished, and she'd arranged for Sadie to collect me and take me back to her house for a while. Other days I'd go home on my own, but today it was kind of a relief that the decision of who to walk with was taken out of my hands.

'Oh. Well, we'll definitely walk to school together tomorrow, okay?'

'Sure,' I said.

'And I'll see you later for Star Club?'

'Yes, see you then!'

Sadie was waiting for me outside the gate, her red car parked just a little way down the hill. She leaned over to give me a hug as I got in the passenger side. 'Hi, honey – how was your first day?'

'Fine,' I said.

'Not too many questions, I hope?'

'Not really,' I said.

'Oh good.'

Sadie started the engine and pulled out of the parking space. I wondered if I should tell her what had happened with Hannah. I didn't want to feel like I was telling tales, but it would be good to talk to someone about it.

'Hannah almost gave me away though,' I said lightly, trying to show I wasn't too concerned. 'She said something about Hollywood and Tracey overheard.'

Sadie frowned. 'I thought Hannah would have been more careful. Who's Tracey? Is that the girl who lives on the other side of you?'

'That's right,' I said. 'I walked to school with her this morning. I was supposed to be going with Hannah but her whole family slept in.'

'Goodness, sounds like Hannah isn't having the best day,' Sadie said. 'So how did Tracey react?'

I gazed out the window, watching the houses rush by. 'I pretended Hannah was just joking. I think Tracey believed me. But maybe I should just tell her, Sadie. She was really nice to me all day, and I'm sure she'd keep my secret if I asked her to.'

'I don't think that's a good idea,' Sadie said firmly. 'The more people you tell the bigger the chance of it all coming out. And what with the project your dad's finishing off at the moment, the least said right now the better.'

'That's true,' I admitted.

'I would leave it for now,' Sadie said. 'After all, you thought you could trust Hannah not to tell anyone, but she almost gave you away today!'

'I *do* trust her — it was just a mistake,' I said. 'I'm sure she'll be more careful next time.'

'Well, why don't you remind them all again, just to be sure,' Sadie said. 'When is your next Star Club meeting?'

'This evening, at 5pm,' I said. 'Can you drop me home for then?'

'Sure thing.' We pulled into Sadie and Grandad's drive-way. 'Now, come on in and have a snack and tell me all about your day.'

Grandad was just taking some scones out of the oven as we came in. 'Hello, poppet. How was your first day?'

'Fine thanks,' I told him. 'Oh Grandad, blackberry scones — my favourite!'

'Made with my own blackberries too,' Grandad told me proudly. 'There aren't many left but you can pick the rest to take home with you later.'

I spread butter on my scone, watching the golden butter melt into the delicious homemade scone, my fingers already stained purple from the blackberries. 'Mmm, delicious!'

'Well, I had to make a Grandad special, it's not every day my granddaughter starts at her mum's old school, now is it!' Grandad said.

'Oh, don't you start,' Sadie warned him. 'Cordelia has been making a song and dance of it already and I think poor Meg is finding it a bit overwhelming.'

Grandad laughed. 'My Meg isn't one to be overwhelmed by something like that, are you, poppet?' He didn't wait for an answer, but, catching Sadie's frown, decided to change the subject. 'What's Doug up to these days then? Is he coming home soon?'

I shook my head, my mouth full of scone. When I'd finished I told him, 'He says he's up to his eyes with the new film. All the promotional work and everything.'

'Stuff and nonsense,' Grandad said gruffly. 'Leave that to the marketing people. In my day actors were actors, and directors were directors, and a film sold itself if it was good enough.'

'Now, John, you know that's not how it works,' Sadie said, helping herself to a scone. 'Your work is very different from Doug's. I'm sure if he says he needs to be there right now he has a good reason.'

Like Sadie and my mum, Grandad is an actor. His spe-
ciality is Shakespeare – he's played all the big parts. He
even named Mum Cordelia after the youngest daughter
in his favourite play, *King Lear*. Cordelia is the loyal, faith-
ful daughter who sticks by her father when her older sisters betray him. Mum doesn't have any older sisters, but
Grandad certainly doesn't have to worry about her betray-
ing him. She adores him, and it's no wonder, because he's
wonderful.

He doesn't have much time for my dad's work, though.
Although Grandad has had a few roles in films over the
years, he much prefers theatre work. Mum is the same. I've
heard so many conversations about it over the years.

'You can't beat the thrill of a live audience,' Grandad
will say. 'Seeing their faces at tense moments in a play –
hearing the applause – there's nothing like it.'

'And that moment when you get a standing ovation for
the first time. Absolutely magic, darling,' Mum will add.

'But you have no record of it!' Dad will say. 'Whereas if
you pull off an amazing performance on TV or film, it's
recorded for all time. People can watch it again and again.'

Grandad will immediately scoff at this. 'What does that
matter? You've had the satisfaction of knowing you've performed well and that the audience have been entertained.
Who cares if it's all recorded on some piece of tape or

on some digital file or something? It's what's in here that counts.' And he taps his head, and then his chest, as if to say his memories are in his heart too.

'And what about when things go wrong?' Dad will say. 'What if you don't have that great performance you're hoping for? When you're filming, you can stop the recording and start again. You can make sure that what goes out to your audience is the best version you can make it.'

'Oh, those endless takes and re-takes!' Mum will moan, putting a hand to her forehead in mock despair. 'I simply can't bear it, darling. Too boring for words. And especially when *you* might have done everything right, but the silly old lighting isn't right, or the sound wasn't switched on or something.'

'Well, at least you have the chance to fix it,' Dad will argue. 'I can't cope with the stress in the theatre, not knowing if the scenery's going to fall over, or my lead actor is going to forget his lines. I want to be able to control what exactly the audience gets to see.'

'You've got to live dangerously in this business,' Grandad will say. 'It gives you an edge, knowing you only have one chance to get it right. People have come to see you tonight and tonight only. You need that adrenalin rush to give it your best shot.'

'I don't want people to see my work for one night only,' Dad will respond. 'And I don't want it to only be seen by people who can afford to go to the theatre. TV and film are for everyone – and not just when it comes out first, but for years and years afterwards.'

Sadie never says much during these discussions, but I can tell she agrees with Mum and Grandad. When you come from a theatrical family, these are the types of conversations you have over the dinner table instead of talking about sports or politics or gossiping about the neighbours.

'Have you got any plays coming up soon, Grandad?' I asked him now.

'*Hamlet* is the next one,' he told me. 'We're hoping to open after Christmas.'

'Oh, are you playing Hamlet?' I asked, excited.

Grandad once played Hamlet in a production that ran for over two years it was so popular. Sadie has the poster framed and hanging on their sitting room wall. Grandad was very handsome and looked every bit the tragic hero.

But Grandad shook his head. 'No, that's a young man's role. I'm going to be Polonius, the advisor to the king. He's a bit of a bumbling, interfering old fool, so I should be just right for the part, eh Sadie?'

'Well, you said it, not me,' Sadie told him, laughing and ruffling his hair affectionately.

'How about doing some rehearsing with me, poppet?' Grandad asked, polishing off the last of his scone. 'You can read Ophelia, Polonius's daughter.'

'Sure,' I said, taking the copy of the script Grandad handed to me and searching for Ophelia's lines.

When I was younger I used to think Shakespeare was so boring. The language was just too difficult and it all went over my head. It was Grandad who got me interested by explaining to me that one of my favourite films, *The Lion King*, is actually based on Hamlet. It's all about a good king who has an evil brother who's jealous of him and wants to be king himself. After that I looked on Shakespeare in a new light, and actually, when you take the time to under-stand the language, the stories are amazing. Already I had been secretly practising the part of Juliet, one of Shake-speare's younger heroines. She was thirteen so only a little older than me. I loved her character and hoped I might get to play her some day.

I didn't know the part of Ophelia so well, but with Grandad's encouragement I threw myself into it. As always happened, I found I was losing myself in the role, home-work and school and worrying about what Hannah had said all forgotten as I thought about Ophelia's worries instead. No wonder I loved acting so much – it was the best form of escapism anyone could want.

Chapter Six

Our Star Club meeting was due to start at 5pm, so Sadie dropped me home just before then. I let myself into the house and dumped my schoolbag in the utility room. Then I went out to the back garden and slipped through the gap in the hedge that Hannah likes to call the secret passage into her garden. Hannah was already there, setting out pens and paper on their garden table.

'Hi, Meg. Did you get your homework done at Sadie's?'

'Yes, it didn't take too long. How about you?'

'Some of it, but I had to leave the rest because Maisie needed help with hers. I'll have to finish later.'

Hannah always seems to help out a lot with her younger brothers and sisters, but especially at the moment because her mum is recovering from a broken ankle. Actually, when it happened it looked like we might have to abandon our plans to put on a show for Maisie's birthday party. Hannah's dad was away in China and her mum really needed her to help look after the younger ones. But I suggested we include the kids in the show instead. It ended up working out really well – Zach and Bobby, who are nine and seven, did some scenes from *Star Wars*, mostly them fighting with lightsabers, which the kids in the audience loved. And Maisie dressed up as a dog and did her own version of 'My Favourite Things'. The only one who wasn't in it was Emma, but she's only a baby.

Thinking back to how much fun we'd had doing the show, I couldn't wait to get started again.

Hannah still looked a bit preoccupied, though. She looked like she wanted to say something, but then she just stopped herself. I wondered if she was still feeling bad about what happened earlier.

'Is everything OK?' I asked her.

'Oh … yes … well, I was just wondering, did you say anything to Tracey about your mum and dad?'

'No – I thought about it, but Sadie doesn't think I should,' I said.

Hannah looked relieved. 'Oh, good. Look, I don't want to put ideas in your head or anything, but the thing about Tracey is …'

Whatever Hannah had been going to say was interrupted when Laura and Ruby appeared in the garden – Zach had let them in through the front door.

'What a day!' Ruby said, flinging her Star Club notebook onto the table and collapsing onto a chair. 'As if it wasn't bad enough having to go the dentist, then we get homework on the very first day. And horrible long division too! That last sum was impossible.'

'Oh no, I still have that to do later,' Hannah groaned. 'I was leaving it until last. Is it going to take me all evening?'

'I didn't think it was too bad,' I said cautiously, wanting to reassure Hannah without insulting Ruby – actually, I'd found it fairly straightforward.

Laura seemed to have no such qualms. 'It was easy!' she said. 'We did those sums all last year.'

'Well, it seems to have all melted out of my brain over the summer,' Ruby said. 'What did you get for the last one?'

'Seventeen, I think it was.'

'WHAT? I got 32.6783.'

We all burst out laughing at Ruby's horrified face.

'OK, enough of long division for the insane,' Hannah said. She sat up straighter in her seat. 'I call this meeting of Star Club to order!'

Hannah always likes to start off our meetings in an official way. She had even done up an agenda – a list of everything we needed to discuss, in the right order.

'So, the first item on our agenda today is to choose a new show,' she said. 'Has anyone got any suggestions?'

'Should we choose something from another book we

like?' Ruby said. 'It worked really well with *Ballet Shoes*.'

'We could, but I thought it would be fun to write some-thing original ourselves this time,' Hannah said. 'Laura, have you got any stories we might be able to use?'

'Weren't you working on something earlier in the summer?' Ruby asked. 'You didn't let us read it. In fact you haven't shown us one of your stories for ages!'

Laura glanced sideways at me, and I smothered a grin. I knew why she hadn't shown us her last story. Over the summer, when I had been trying not to talk about my dad so I wouldn't have to lie to my new friends about where he was working, I had taken the secrecy a bit too far. Laura had got it into her head that my parents were involved in a custody battle over me, that my mum had run away with me to Carrickbeg and that my dad was going to try to find me and kidnap me. Laura has a wild imagination, which is great for writing stories, but not always so good for handling real life. She'd let her imagi-nation run away with her that time all right. She'd even written a story based on what was going on, though when she found out the truth she absolutely refused to let any of us see it – I think she was pretty embarrassed about the whole thing.

'I didn't finish that one,' she said, giving a slight cough. 'I've started a new one instead, but it's going to take me a while to make some progress with it. I think it would be better to just adapt another story so we can get started quickly.'

This was exactly the right argument to win Hannah over – she definitely didn't want any delays with us getting started. 'OK, let's do that then. What should we do?'

'How about adapting a fairytale?' I suggested. 'A sort of modern-day version of one, maybe?'

'That could be good fun!' Hannah said. 'And it would still be original if we were doing a new version of one. My favourite was always Snow White and the Seven Dwarves.'

'Too many parts in that one,' Laura pointed out. 'There are only four of us!'

'Good point,' Hannah said. 'Snow White and the Three Dwarves doesn't sound quite as good really! Well, how about Goldilocks and the Three Bears? There are four parts in that.'

'I'm not sure how we could make it modern though,' Laura said, putting her head on one side to think.

'Maybe the bears could be eating bagels and cream cheese instead of porridge,' Ruby giggled.

'And they could have reclining chairs instead of arm-chairs,' I joined in.

'OK, I'm not sure that's going to work,' Hannah said, tapping her pen on her notebook. 'Let's have a think for a few minutes – and don't suggest something unless you can think of how we can modernise it!'

I saw Laura and Ruby exchanging quick smiles. Hannah was in full-on Star Club director mode and wasn't in the mood for any messing! She didn't notice the smiles, gazing into space as she tried to come up with an idea. Hannah was a great director, I thought, a bit like my dad, and some other directors I'd seen over the years, totally focused on making things happen.

We were quiet for a few minutes, thinking. Then, tentatively, I put forward my own childhood favourite. 'How about Cinderella? It doesn't have too many parts, and it should be easy to do a modern version. Cinderella could be going to a disco instead of a ball.'

'That's a great idea,' Hannah said, beaming. 'That could work really well. Let's just think about the parts and see if it would work. We've got Cinderella, the two ugly stepsisters, the fairy godmother and the stepmother.'

'Don't forget the prince,' Ruby giggled.

'Maybe that's too many parts,' Hannah said, frowning. 'I don't really want to have to get anyone else involved this time. It would be nice to do something just the four of us.'

'We can double up on parts like we did last time,' I said. 'Laura did a great job of switching between Madame Fidolia and Nana.'

Hannah's face brightened. 'That's true. It could work if we just plan out the scenes properly.'

'Have you got a copy of the story?' Laura asked. 'I'm not

sure if I remember it properly.'

'I'm sure Maisie has a copy somewhere,' Hannah said, jumping to her feet. 'I know I've read it to her often enough. I'll go and see.'

'Well, don't tell her what you want it for,' Laura warned. 'She'll only want to be one of Cinderella's mice or something.'

'Oh God, that's a good point,' Hannah said. 'I'll just sneak it out without saying anything.'

When we were rehearsing *Ballet Shoes* last summer, Maisie had kept pestering Hannah to let her be the dog. Even though there is no dog in *Ballet Shoes*. She got her chance in the end when we turned our performance into a variety show, and she had done a fantastic job. But I knew Hannah wouldn't want her trying to take part in Cinderella – she seemed quite keen on making it just the four of us this time, which I could understand.

Hannah came back with a huge hardback copy of collected Disney stories. 'This one was in the playroom,' she said, putting it down on the table with a thud. 'I know we've got the old Ladybird version too, but it's in our room and Maisie's in there so I can't smuggle it out without her asking me a million questions.'

'This one should be fine, the story is basically the same,' I said. I started flicking through the pages to find the right story.

'Should we try to do the whole story, or just pick out a few key scenes like we did with *Ballet Shoes*?' Laura wondered.

'Let's do the whole thing. It would make more sense,' Hannah said.

'Oooh, wouldn't it be fun to do it as a pantomime?' Ruby exclaimed. 'I saw it in the Gaiety once and it was brilliant. We could have singing and dancing then too – and the pantomime dame would be so much fun to do – you could play her, Laura!'

Laura immediately took offence to this suggestion, not impressed that Ruby thought she would be convincing as an elderly, overweight, comic figure who is usually played by a man. Ruby rushed to reassure her that this wasn't what she meant at all. As they were squabbling, my mind was whirling with the thought of us putting on a whole pantomime ourselves. We could have a whole chorus of dancers and singers and the jokes you always get with pantomimes would be fun to write and to act. Maybe Grandad could make us some scenery so we'd have a proper set!

'OK, I think we're getting a bit ahead of ourselves here,' said Hannah, always the practical one. 'We'd need way more than four people to do a pantomime. You're probably talking about more like twenty! I'd love to try it some day, but I think we should start off a bit smaller. This is only our second show – we shouldn't make things too hard for ourselves.'

Hannah's sensible approach brought me back to earth. She was right of course – we didn't want to take on too much. And anyway, this way I'd get to focus on the bit I really loved – bringing a character to life.

'When you two are quite finished,' Hannah said, sounding almost like a teacher as she frowned at Laura and Ruby, who were still arguing, 'let's take it in turns to read a bit of the story and maybe it will give us some ideas. Cinderella has been done so many times I think we need to do something a bit different or people will just find it too unoriginal. I'll read the first bit then.'

I passed the book to Hannah and sat back to listen to her reading. There was a time when, just like Maisie, I almost knew the story off by heart, and I found it all coming back to me as Hannah read. The ugly stepmother who makes Cinderella work so hard, the horrible stepsisters who are so mean to her, the fairy godmother who comes along and saves the day, the handsome prince who falls in love with the mysterious girl at the ball and finds her glass slipper. It was such a great story, I could never get tired of it.

We passed it around the table to read. As I listened to the others reading I tried to think of ways we could change the story to make it more modern. I was last to read, so I got the nice bit where Cinderella tries on the shoe and the prince realises he's found his true love. Even though I'm old enough now to realise that not many people decide they're going to marry someone after dancing with them for five minutes, I still love that bit. I'm a sucker for a happy ending.

'So what do you think we could do to make the story modern?' Hannah said, all business-like again. 'I really like the idea of doing a disco instead of the ball, but what about the rest?'

'Would we still have the magic part in it?' Ruby wondered. 'You know, when the fairy godmother turns the pumpkin into the carriage and Cinderella's rags into a ballgown.'

'That must be pretty tricky to do on stage,' Laura said.

I thought back to when I'd seen a pantomime version of Cinderella. They'd cleverly managed the magic bits with lighting and a mist that rose up at just the right time. Mum explained that the stagehands were able to quickly wheel the huge carriage (which was just a cut-out, not a real carriage) onto the stage, hiding the pumpkin. I was mystified by Cinderella's quick costume change though until Mum told me there were actually two actresses involved – the actress playing Cinderella had a double who appeared on stage just for a moment wearing the rags, not long enough for the audience to realise she wasn't the real one, and then the mist allowed them to swap places, with the real actress having changed into a beautiful ballgown.

I explained all this to my friends. Hannah was thrilled to hear all the detail – as our director, she always likes to know the ins and outs of what goes on backstage.

'I don't really see how we could manage that ourselves though,' she said reluctantly. 'We don't even have lighting, let alone a mist machine!'

We all thought for a minute, then Laura had a brilliant idea. 'How about ...' she said slowly, 'instead of a fairy god-mother who works magic, we have a cool aunt who gives Cinderella a makeover. She can do her hair and make-up, and buy her a new dress for the disco.'

'Oh I love it!' I said. 'That sounds perfect!'

'And maybe instead of losing her shoe at the ball, Cinderella could lose her handbag at the disco!' Hannah said.

'Yes! And then the handsome boy she meets has to try to track her down,' said Laura.

'We have to keep the mean stepsisters though!' Ruby said. 'The story wouldn't be the same without them!'

'Well, lots of people do have stepsisters they don't get on with,' I said. 'And sisters too ...'

'Yes, let's keep the stepsisters,' Hannah said. 'But we could probably skip the stepmother, couldn't we? If we're doing it a different way anyway, and it's all about going to a disco. It would mean one less part to have to double up on.'

'That makes sense,' I said. 'So we'd have scenes with

Cinderella and the stepsisters, then Cinderella and the cool aunt, and then the disco scene would have to have Cinderella and the sisters and the handsome boy.'

'So one person could play the cool aunt and the handsome boy, because they're not in the same scene,' Laura finished.

'We'll just need a clever costume change then if we're having the same person in both parts!' I said. 'Like maybe even a wig or something?'

'I hate to interrupt your meeting, but have you girls seen the time?' It was Hannah's mum, Claire, standing at the back door with baby Emma on her hip. 'Ruby, didn't you say your mum wanted you home by six?'

'Thanks, Claire, I hadn't realised the time,' Ruby said. 'I'd better go, you guys.'

Claire went back inside and Ruby and Laura began gathering up their things.

'OK, so why don't we all have a think about it over the next few days and on Friday we can start planning out the scenes and see who's going to play who?' Hannah said.

'Sounds good to me,' said Ruby. 'We can meet at my house on Friday.'

I took a deep breath. 'Could I just say something before we finish up? It's just about Mum and Dad's jobs and all that.' Hannah immediately turned scarlet again and looked down at the ground. I rushed on, wanting to get it over with so I didn't embarrass her any more than necessary. 'I'm not getting at you Hannah, honest. I know it was a mistake. I just wanted to remind everyone to please be careful not to say anything. I just want a chance to get to know people at school before I tell them. I mean, I'm so glad I got to know you guys before you found out. Admit it, you'd have thought of me differently if you were introduced to me as the daughter of an actress and a film director.'

Laura always tells it like it is. 'We probably would,' she said. 'And I'm sure Star Club wouldn't have worked out the way it has.'

'We'd have had to make you the director instead of Hannah,' Ruby giggled.

'And that would have been a disaster!' I said. 'I love acting but I'm really not interested in directing.'

Hannah's blushes were starting to fade. 'I really do understand, Meg. It was a total mistake today, and I'll be much more careful from now on.'

She was still looking at me warily as if she expected me to bite her head off again. Impulsively, I reached over and hugged her. 'Thanks Hannah, I know you will. You're a great friend – you all are!'

'Group hug!' cried Ruby, and we all threw our arms around each other, giggling.

'OK, see you on Friday in Ruby's house,' Hannah said.

'And we'll get started properly. Yay – it's going to be great doing a new show!'

Hannah went to see Laura and Ruby out the front way, while I made my way to the gap in the hedge. I glanced back to watch my friends leave, thinking again how lucky it was that I had got to know them as just me. Because the thing was, I had another secret, one that even my Star Club friends didn't know about yet.

Chapter Seven

A delicious spicy smell hit me as soon as I opened the back door. Mum was standing at the cooker, stirring something in a saucepan and humming to herself. Clearly her domestic goddess thing was still going strong.

'Meg, darling! How was your first day?' Mum flung the wooden spoon down any old way and threw her arms around me. 'I'm so sorry I wasn't there to collect you, but I simply couldn't leave early after being off all last week. My boss just can't seem to manage without me.'

Mum works in an office in town. I'm still not entirely sure what she does, except that it involves using some complicated computer program that she had to bluff her way through to get the job. Luckily bluffing comes easily to Mum.

Mum ushered me over to the kitchen table, still talking. 'Come and sit down, darling, and tell me all about it. What's your teacher like? Was Sadie there on time? Did she give you a snack? How's Grandad getting on with Polonius?'

'Slow down, Mum,' I said, laughing. 'That's a lot of questions. I feel like I'm back in school!'

Mum laughed. 'Sorry, darling. Well, just tell me how you got on, I'm dying to hear.'

I hesitated, wondering where to start. 'Uh – it was fine, really. Our teacher is called Miss Brennan, and she's very nice. A bit strict about talking in class, but I guess most teachers are.'

'And who are you sitting beside?'

'I'm sitting beside Tracey, the girl from next door. I walked to school with her this morning.' I wondered if Mum would ask why I hadn't walked with Hannah, but she just seemed pleased that I was meeting more people.

'Oh, how nice!' Mum clapped her hands together. 'You're making new friends already. I knew you'd get on just fine! And how did you get on with the schoolwork? I hope you weren't too far behind!'

'I don't think so,' I said. 'The maths was OK, anyway. And I felt like my Irish was coming back to me once we started some reading.'

'Oh to be young,' Mum sighed. 'Your brain is just like a little sponge, ready to soak everything up! I feel like I've already forgotten most of what I ever learnt.'

Suddenly I realised that the lovely spicy smell had been

replaced by a nasty one. 'Mum – is something burning?' I asked.

'My dhal!' exclaimed Mum. She ran to the cooker and grabbed the saucepan, moving it off the ring. As soon as she took off the lid steam came rushing out and the putrid smell started to fill the whole kitchen.

'Oh no, it's ruined!' Mum wailed. 'And I spent ages grating fresh ginger and everything. Open the door, Meg. I'm going to throw it into the garden before the whole house is filled with the smell – it's simply appalling!'

I opened the door, and Mum threw the dhal, saucepan and all, into the garden. She banged the door shut and the two of us stood for a moment looking at it as it steamed quietly away in the grass. Then Mum caught my eye and the two of us burst into giggles.

'So, how about eating out to celebrate your first day of school?' Mum suggested. 'I've been meaning to try that new diner on the main road.'

'Excellent plan,' I told her. 'I really didn't feel like dhal anyway.'

Later that evening, Dad Skyped us to see how my first day had gone. I knew Mum had probably texted him to remind him. Dad is not great at remembering things like that on his own, especially not when he's in the middle of one of his projects. I didn't mind, though. It was lovely that he wanted to talk to me, even if he seemed a bit distracted.

'How's my favourite girl?' he asked, shading his eyes so he could see the screen better in the bright California sunshine. It looked like he was sitting on the balcony of his hotel room – in the background I could see palm trees framed against a clear blue sky. For a moment I wished I could be back in LA, feeling the sun soaking into my skin and the sand between my toes as I walked along a beautiful beach. I thought of strolling along the boardwalk at Venice Beach, stopping to look at the stalls or watch some of the street performers, and the smells of exotic food from all the cafes nearby.

'Fine,' I said. 'I survived my first day, anyway!'

'Of course you did!' Dad said. 'I just hope that school realise how lucky they are to have such a special girl in their midst! So when are you coming out to visit? You must have a mid-term break coming up soon?'

'Don't be silly, Doug.' Mum was calling across the kitchen from where she was drying the dishes – Dad couldn't see her, but I had no doubt that he could hear her. 'She's only just started!'

'Oh well, I suppose you might need a few weeks to settle in,' Dad said, rolling his eyes at me as if he and I were conspiring against Mum. 'But it would be fantastic to get you out here after that, help me out with some publicity for the new film!'

Mum dropped the tea towel and came marching over

the table to stand behind me. I saw her appear suddenly in the small picture on the screen showing our side of the conversation, and Dad immediately leaned back in his chair, almost as if she had just lunged towards him in real life.

'Now don't start this again, Doug!' Mum said, sounding really cross. 'You know what we agreed! Meg is twelve years old and she's had more than enough of Hollywood for now. She's perfectly happy here with her new school and her friends and we're settling down to a normal family life for a while.'

'But she's a natural,' Dad argued. 'You can't keep her away from it, Cordelia. You saw what happened as soon as you moved home – she's joined that little drama club, and straight away they're putting on that wonderful show, which I've no doubt was mostly Meg's work!'

I wanted to step in and say that it hadn't been at all – Hannah was our director, and she was brilliant at organising everyone and making the whole production work smoothly. All I wanted to do was act – I was quite happy to leave everything else to other people, whether that was directing, or planning, or all this publicity work Dad seemed to want me to be involved in. But I couldn't get a word in between Mum and Dad, and I knew Dad would believe what he wanted to believe anyway.

'You're talking nonsense as usual, Doug!' Mum said, her

voice becoming shriller. 'Of course Meg is free to enjoy her drama club with her friends! That's a completely different thing from what you have in mind and you know it!'

'Just a week or two, Cordelia – what harm could it do?' Dad pleaded.

'Absolutely not!' Mum said. 'We've done it your way long enough, and now we're doing it my way for a while.'

Do I get any say in this, I wondered?

'What about what Meg wants?' Dad asked, as if reading my mind. 'You'd love to come back out here, wouldn't you honey?'

'Now don't start trying to make her choose between us!' Mum said. 'That's a cheap trick and you know it!'

I got up from my chair. 'If you two are just going to argue I may as well go and finish my homework!' I said. 'I thought Dad was calling to see how I got on in my first day at school, not so you can argue about the same old things over and over again!'

'Meg, wait!' Dad called, and Mum reached out a hand to me, but I stormed off.

In my room, I took out one of my school books and pretended to be studying just in case Mum came after me, but in reality my mind was far away. Mum wanted me to be ordinary. Dad wanted me to be extraordinary. But what did I want to be?

Chapter Eight

Next morning Tracey was waiting for me in the driveway, ready to walk to school together.

'Hi Meg – let's get going, will we?'

'I said I'd wait for Hannah,' I told her. 'We can all walk down together when she comes.'

'Oh, you don't want to wait for Hannah,' Tracey said. 'You know what she's like – she'll have lost her homework or the baby will have spilled porridge all over her. Or they're all still in bed!' She rolled her eyes. 'Come on, we don't want to be late.'

'I'd better wait for her,' I said, feeling a bit uncomfortable. 'I said I would. I'm sure she won't be long.'

'Oh well, if you'd rather walk with her than me ...' Tracey said, tossing her hair over her shoulder and stalking off before I could say anything else.

I stared after Tracey, wondering what had gotten into her. Why couldn't we all just walk to school together?

Hannah came running out of her house, her schoolbag flapping behind her. 'Hi Meg! I'm not late, am I? I set my own alarm today just in case!'

'No, you're fine,' I told her.

Tracey had already passed Ruby's house, taking absolutely no notice of Ruby who was sitting on her wall waiting for us, and was almost at the entrance to Woodland Green. I was about to tell Hannah how odd she was being, but Hannah started talking first.

'So Maisie caught me reading *Cinderella* and now she's convinced we need her for the show!' she said. 'She wants to be one of the birds that helps Cinderella make her ball-gown.'

'Oh, I can just picture her!' I said, imagining Maisie prancing around the stage flapping her wings and adjusting Cinderella's dress. 'I bet she'd love a costume covered in feathers.'

'Don't give her any ideas!' Hannah warned. 'I've told her she's not being in it. I'd like a slightly more peaceful experience this time!'

Ruby jumped down from the wall as we reached her house. 'Hi you guys! So did anyone else have Cinderella nightmares last night?'

'Uhhh – no …' said Hannah. 'What happened?'

Ruby fell into step beside us. 'I dreamt I was being chased through a forest by a giant glass slipper! I tried to escape by climbing an enormous pumpkin, but it was too slippery and I kept sliding off!'

'Oh my God, if you're already having anxiety dreams about the show what are you going to be like when we're actually ready to go on stage?' Hannah giggled.

'Who knows? Mum says I'm going to have to start drinking some camomile tea or something to calm myself down,' Ruby said.

When we got to school I started worrying again that Tracey was going to be weird towards me, but when I slid into my seat beside her she was all smiles, as if nothing had happened. 'Did you manage to get your homework done?' she asked. 'I hope those sums weren't too tricky for you.'

'No, it was fine thanks,' I said.

'Oh good, well if you need any help just let me know!' Tracey smiled sweetly at me before turning to talk to Jamie on the other side. I'd noticed that they seemed to get on well, and were always whispering together. Feeling relieved that everything seemed OK between us, I took out my pencil case and listened as Miss Brennan began going through last night's maths homework.

* * *

When Sadie collected me from school that day, I told her all about the plans for our new show. I already knew who

I wanted to be – one of the ugly stepsisters. I wasn't interested in Cinderella, even though it would be the biggest part and she'd get to wear the nicest costumes. I found the idea of a character part much more appealing. I'd have a chance to make my stepsister really comical and get some great reactions from the audience.

With *Ballet Shoes*, it had been really easy to choose our own roles. Ruby was the obvious choice for Posy, the youngest sister, as they're both crazy about ballet. Hannah was really keen on playing Pauline – she felt she had a lot in common with her because they both wanted to be actresses. I loved Pauline too, but I was much more attracted to Petrova's role – I just found her such an interesting character, because she was forced to train for the stage even though all she wanted to do was mess about with car engines and watch planes. She was pretty much the opposite of me, and I loved the idea of that challenge.

Laura took on the roles of both Madame Fidolia, who ran the theatre school the girls attended, and Nana who looked after them. She was great – she seemed to love the chance to play two such different parts, and she switched between the two with no trouble at all. She seemed like the obvious choice to play the cool aunt and the handsome boy.

Sadie loved the idea of a modern-day Cinderella. 'You can have such fun with that,' she said. 'I can't wait to see what you come up with.'

Mum was enthusiastic too, suggesting all sorts of accessories she could lend us for our costumes.

But when I called Dad to tell him, he didn't seem to be very interested. 'That's nice, honey,' he said. 'I don't suppose you've had any luck in talking Mum around, have you?'

'About what?' I asked, confused.

'About letting you come back out to LA, of course,' Dad said, sounding impatient. 'I could really do with your help.'

'Oh, that ...' I twisted a strand of hair around my finger, wondering what to say. The thing was, I was actually quite glad Mum had put her foot down. Even though I'd loved our time in California, I wasn't in any rush to go back there, especially when all Dad wanted me for was to help him with the promotional work for his film. I had too much going on here – new house, new school, and a new show to plan with Star Club. And even though I didn't like to admit that Mum was right, it did feel quite nice to be ordinary for a while.

How could I explain all that to Dad, though? He was so wrapped up in his film he couldn't understand that it wasn't the centre of my world like it was his. 'I don't think Mum is going to give in,' I said at last, taking the easy option of blaming Mum. I felt a bit bad – but only a bit.

Mum was well able to stand up to Dad if she needed to. I didn't have her strength.

Dad sighed. 'I was afraid you were going to say that. Maybe I need to come home, try to talk her around in person. What do you think?'

'Maybe you should leave it for a little while,' I said, feeling torn. It would be so great to see Dad – but not if he and Mum were just going to argue.

'Well, I can't this week anyway,' Dad said, suddenly sounding full of energy again. 'I've got the meeting with the PR agency to go through the photos, another meeting with the media manager to set up some interviews, and I have to run through some numbers for our finance guy. And that's just Thursday! Actually, I'd better go now, honey. I have a lunch with the producer, and I'm just back from the gym so I need to hop in the shower. Good luck with Rapunzel!'

He didn't even wait for me to say goodbye before hanging up. I gazed at the phone, which still showed his photo, one I'd taken on holidays which showed him tanned and laughing at something I'd said. And now he couldn't even be bothered remembering the name of my show.

* * *

All week, I found myself daydreaming about Cinderella

any chance I got. I found my special Ladybird copy of *Cinderella* that my aunt Margaret, who I'm named after, had had made specially for my birthday when I was four. It had the same storyline and illustrations as the copy Mum had had when she was a child, but the main character was called Meg instead of Cinderella. I loved that book so much and made Mum read it for me every night for weeks.

I felt a slight pang of regret that we weren't doing the real story of Cinderella. I pictured myself dressed as one of the ugly stepsisters with a poudré wig, beauty spot strategically placed near my mouth, and a puffy, extravagant ballgown, looking ridiculously overdone compared to Cinderella's innocent beauty.

I wondered for a minute if I should try to talk the others into doing the original Cinderella after all. But when I thought about it I realised Hannah was right – everyone knew the story so well, and with just the four of us it would be hard to manage scenes like the ball. And that was before we even thought about the lighting and special effects and how we'd manage the magic. We could do it of course, but it wouldn't be as professional as we wanted. I felt we had a lot to live up to after our amazing variety show in the summer. People would be expecting something a bit special.

Anyway, it would be fun to create a new storyline ourselves. I cheered up at the thought of the fun we'd have making the story our own. We could dress the stepsisters in crazy, over-the-top outfits – clashing patterns and stripes, luminous oranges and greens, fluffy pink feather boas and strings of beads. They'd have to wear too much make-up, of course – thick orange foundation and maybe even false eyelashes. I wondered if Hannah's mum would let her – she seemed a bit strict about letting Hannah do a lot of things, as if she didn't want her growing up too fast, but maybe she wouldn't mind when it was just for a show.

I realised I was jumping a bit too far ahead. I was already thinking about Hannah as the other ugly stepsister along with me. In fact I didn't even know if I'd get to be a step-sister – maybe Laura or Ruby would want to play one of them. We hadn't talked properly about who was going to play who. Hannah was quite strict about keeping decisions like that to our proper Star Club meetings. So even though we'd chatted about the show at break time at school and on our walks home, we'd stayed away from discussing cast-ing. Hannah thought we should have a few days' 'thinking time' first, and we'd all agreed that was a good idea.

But even though no one had said anything, it seemed to me like we had a natural fit for each role. Ruby was the perfect choice for Cinderella. She was smaller than the rest of us, slightly built with her dancer's frame, and with delicate features. She would look just the part as the downtrodden, lonely girl being bullied by her stepsisters. I could picture her sitting by the fire lost in her dreams of escaping a life of drudgery – or whatever we decided to have instead of a fire!

Hannah would make a brilliant stepsister along with me. We'd had a lot of scenes together in *Ballet Shoes* and we had played really well off each other – we seemed to bring out the best in each other. And Laura could be the cool aunt and the handsome boy – that's if she didn't mind having to juggle two parts again.

It was so much fun making all these plans, and I couldn't wait for our meeting on Friday.

Chapter Nine

Things were a bit weird with Tracey. I tried calling for her on Thursday morning to walk to school, but no one answered the doorbell, even though I saw the curtains twitching. I called for Hannah and Ruby instead and we all walked down together.

When we were sitting together in the classroom though, Tracey was really friendly. She asked me if I wanted to come over to her house later.

'We could play some computer games,' she said. 'I've got this new one my dad bought me when we were in Florida. He always buys me the newest games. It's not even out over here yet for another few weeks.'

I wasn't sure what to say. I didn't want to offend Tracey, but I wasn't really into computer games. Then I remembered I'd promised to go over to Hannah's. 'Uh, thanks, Tracey, but I said I'd go over to Hannah's. Maybe another time.'

Tracey's smile disappeared. 'Well, of course if you'd rather go over to Hannah's house that's fine. I'm surprised she's got time to have friends over, what with minding all those brothers and sisters. But her mum probably thought it was no big deal for her to mind one more person.'

'What do you mean?' I asked, not understanding.

'Well, it's kind of obvious, isn't it?' Tracey said. 'I mean, of course her mum would expect her to mind the new girl. She's that kind of interfering mum who'd make Hannah look after someone whether she really wanted to be friends with them or not.'

'I'm sure it's not like that,' I said, my voice wobbling a little.

'I'd just hate to see you get hurt, Meg,' Tracey said, patting my arm. 'You know, when you're not new any more and Hannah doesn't feel like she has to mind you.'

I said nothing. Was that really what had happened?

Tracey leaned in closer to me. 'Look, I didn't want to have to tell you this … no, I'd better not say anything.'

'What?' I asked.

'It's just that Hannah – no, I really shouldn't say anything.' Tracey pursed up her lips, as if stopping herself from saying any more.

'Hannah what?'

Tracey looked all around to check no one was listening, then put her head right in beside mine. 'Hannah's been saying all sorts of nasty things about you.'

A sick feeling washed over me. I didn't want to believe Tracey, but why would she make it up? 'Like what?'

Tracey shook her head. 'I couldn't repeat it. I hate people who spread gossip, don't you? Anyway, I know it couldn't possibly be true.'

'Tracey, you can't just say something like that and not tell me what she said,' I insisted, trying to keep my voice from shaking.

But Tracey just shook her head again. 'I'm sorry, Meg. I shouldn't have said anything at all. I don't want to cause any trouble, but I couldn't stand back and watch you let Hannah use you like that. She's not really your friend at all. I could tell you all sorts of things about her, but like I said, I'm not one to gossip.'

Across the classroom, Hannah, Laura and Ruby were working on their project together, heads bent over the table, talking and giggling. Surely Hannah wasn't capable of saying nasty things about me behind my back. It just didn't seem possible. Was Tracey making it all up, and if so, why?

She looked at me, an innocent expression in her big blue eyes, and I really didn't know what to think.

* * *

Later, I told Mum what Tracey had said. Like I could have predicted, Mum immediately went into protective mother-hen mode.

'What a strange thing for her to say! Did she tell you what Hannah is supposed to have said?'

'No, she wouldn't tell me,' I said. 'She said she didn't want to cause any trouble.'

Mum gave one of her explosive snorts. She has a whole collection, and this was her most derisory one. 'But that's exactly what she's doing, darling! Honestly, I find it hard to imagine Hannah saying anything nasty about anyone, least of all you! She's such a nice, sincere girl, and you two are such great friends. I'm quite sure it's nothing but a load of old cobblers, darling.'

It was such a relief to hear Mum saying what I thought myself. 'I'm so glad you think that, Mum. That's what I thought too, but I was a bit upset about it.'

'Well of course, darling. It's impossible not to be upset when one hears something like that. All sorts of things start running through one's head, don't they?' Mum frowned. 'What can Tracey possibly have been thinking? Do she and Hannah not get along?'

'I haven't really seen them together much,' I said. 'It's almost like they're avoiding each other.'

'Perhaps there's a bit of history there,' Mum said. 'Girls' friendships can be so tricky.'

'I just don't know why Tracey would say something like that,' I said, still hoping for some kind of answer. 'She seems to think Hannah's not really my friend – that she was only looking after me because I'm new.'

'What nonsense!' Mum said. 'Anyone can see the two of you get on like a house on fire – not to mention the rest of your little gang. Please don't worry about Tracey, darling. In my experience the most common reason for that type of behaviour is one thing and one thing alone. Jealousy.'

'Oh Mum, you always think people are jealous of me. It's a mum thing,' I laughed. Mum always seems to think I'm the prettiest, cleverest and generally most interesting person in any group I happen to be in. I'm pretty sure all mums think the same thing about their own children.

'Not jealous of you, darling, though I'm quite sure that's a possibility too. Jealous of Hannah, I mean. Because it sounds to me like Tracey really wants to have your friend-ship all to herself.'

I let this idea sink in for a minute, wondering if Mum could really be on to something. Why would Tracey so desperately want to be friends with me?

Chapter Ten

By the time Friday came along I'd managed to put it out of my head and was only thinking about our rehearsal. We met in Ruby's garden right after school.

'Hurray for Friday and no homework!' Ruby said, pouring everyone a big glass of strawberry smoothie her mum had made specially for our meeting.

'Yes, thank goodness that's over. The first week back at school just seems like it lasts forever, doesn't it?' Laura said.

'Oh, I thought it was just me!' I said. 'You know, with not having been to school for a while. I thought I was just finding it hard to adjust to sitting at a desk all day.'

'How did it work when you were in LA?' Hannah asked. 'Did your tutor come to your apartment?'

'Sometimes she did, and sometimes we'd be on the film set and I'd have lessons in between takes,' I said. I stopped, wondering if I'd said too much, then added quickly, 'I mean, if Mum was doing a full day of acting, and she didn't want to leave me at home all day. My tutor and I would go to the studio or wherever they were filming, and I'd do some lessons in the dressing room or the trailer. Then I could watch some of the filming too.'

'That must have been so cool,' Hannah said with a wistful sigh. 'I'd love to watch a film being made.'

'Some of it is pretty boring,' I said honestly. 'There's a lot of doing the same thing over and over. But there are always new people to meet and production guys running here and there. And the food! Oh wow, you should just see the snack trolleys.'

'A bit different from lunch time in school I bet,' Ruby said with a laugh. 'I'm sick of packed lunches already. This was a long week – I felt like the weekend would NEVER come!'

'I think everyone feels like that the first week,' Laura said.

'And plenty of other weeks too,' Hannah said, which made us laugh.

'Anyway, the weekend's here now, so YAY!' said Ruby. 'Cheers, everyone!' She raised her glass of smoothie in the air and we all clinked glasses.

I smiled around at my friends, feeling a warm glow that I was part of such a close group. I didn't know if they realised just how important they were to me. The fact was it was ages since I'd made any new friends. Actually, if I'm being honest, it was ages since I'd had any friends at all. That's a really sad thing for a twelve-year-old girl to admit, isn't it? Sad, as in pathetic, though I suppose it's pretty sad in a boohoo, woe is me sort of sense as well. But then I'm not exactly an average twelve-year-old as Dad always likes to remind me. I know Mum would like me to be, though. But hanging around on a film set, having lessons with a tutor instead of going to school, means the chance to make friends isn't really there. I thought of some of the kids I'd been friendly with in my school in New York, and before that in Dublin. It would have been great to stay in contact with them, but we were all too young to have our own phones or email or anything like that, and my family was always on the move, so we'd kind of lost touch. I was determined that whatever happened now I'd stay friends with Ruby, Laura and Hannah.

'So should we start with the cast list, or with the storyline?' Hannah asked, opening her notebook.

'Cast list, cast list!' Ruby and Laura chorused.

'OK – how are we going to decide?' Hannah asked. 'I don't feel like we have such obvious choices as we did last time.'

'Don't you?' I asked in surprise. 'I do. I've been thinking about it all week and I keep picturing us all in certain parts.'

'Me too,' Laura said.

'I just keep picturing myself in all the parts and wanting to play them all,' Hannah admitted. 'That's a sign of a good story I suppose! Well, why don't you tell us what you were thinking then, Meg?'

'OK – well, I think Ruby would be great as Cinderella,' I said.

'Oh NO!' Ruby protested at once. 'I thought you'd be Cinderella, Meg. I couldn't play her.'

'Why not?' I asked, surprised at her reaction. I had been so sure that Ruby would love to be Cinderella.

'I thought of Ruby for Cinderella too,' Laura said. 'You look just right for the part.'

'But it's the biggest part in the show,' Ruby said, looking worried. 'I just don't know if I'd manage to learn the lines.'

This was something I hadn't thought of. Of all of us, Ruby was the one who had struggled the most with learning her lines in the last show. We'd worked hard to help her and by the time performance day came around she was absolutely fine. But would giving her the principal role be too risky?

'Oh, you'd be fine,' Hannah said, though she didn't sound completely sure. 'But you don't have to if you don't want to. Is there another part you'd prefer?'

'I thought maybe I could be the handsome boy,' Ruby said. 'I'd like the chance to play a boy. I think I could convey the part well using movement, you know? It's something we do in ballet exercises sometimes.'

'But you're much smaller than any of us,' Laura said. 'Wouldn't it look weird that Cinderella was way taller than the prince? Or handsome boy, I mean!'

'I don't think that matters,' Ruby said, sounding kind of stubborn. 'So what if the boy is smaller? Anyway, it sounds like a much shorter part so I think I could manage it OK.'

'But Ruby, whoever plays the boy has to play the cool aunt as well,' Hannah pointed out. 'Remember, we worked out that's the way we'd do it because they're not in the same scenes.'

'Oh, right, I'd forgotten that.' Ruby looked anxious. 'Well, maybe I could do Cinderella then – I'm not sure.'

'What about the ugly stepsisters?' Hannah asked. 'Who did you have in mind for those, Meg?'

'Well, don't take this personally, but I thought maybe you and I could play them,' I told her. 'Even though it would obviously be extremely difficult to make ourselves ugly enough.'

Hannah laughed. 'I'm glad you added that bit. I'd be happy with that, I think we'd make a good pair.' She smiled at me, and I beamed back, thrilled that she liked the idea of us working as a pair. Tracey had definitely got it wrong, I decided. Of course Hannah was my friend.

Laura groaned. 'I suppose that means you want me to be the one doing two parts again.'

'Well, that's what I thought, but of course you don't have to if you don't want to.' I glanced around the group, feeling a bit anxious. It seemed like only Hannah and I were really happy with the parts I'd suggested. Was our show about to fall apart before we'd even started?

Hannah was obviously feeling concerned too. 'We could just put all the parts into a hat, and take whichever one we pick out?' she suggested. 'Or, you know, we could always pick a different story to do if people think this one's not right for us?'

Laura gave Hannah a fake punch. 'I'm only joking, silly! I'm actually happy with two parts – it stops me getting bored of one! And it's fun coming up with completely different looks for the two.'

We all looked at Ruby, who blushed and said shyly, 'Well, if you really want me to be Cinderella, I'll do it. Just don't make my lines too long, OK?'

'Brilliant!' exclaimed Hannah. 'That's settled then. Now we can get on with planning the scenes!'

'Are you sure, Ruby?' I asked her quietly. I didn't want her to feel pressured into it. That was no way to start off a big part.

But Ruby nodded firmly. 'Yes, it's good to challenge myself! Anyway, I've just remembered that Cinderella is a ballet too, so it will be good to get the practice if I want to be a prima ballerina some day!'

'Oh well, it's perfect for you so!' I said, exchanging glances with Hannah. I could tell she was also wondering how playing a modern-day Cinderella would help Ruby to dance the part in a ballet some day, but if it made her feel more positive about the role that had to be a good thing. Maybe I could help her work on her lines and find an easy way to bring the part to life.

'OK, so scenes!' Hannah said. 'Let's start with the step-sisters being mean to Cinderella – and let's make them as horrible as we possibly can!'

The rest of our meeting flew by and I couldn't believe it was six o'clock already when Ruby's dad came out to tell her dinner was ready and it was time for the rest of us to go home.

'Let's meet up again tomorrow,' Hannah suggested. 'What time is your ballet class, Ruby?'

'It's at ten, so any time after eleven would be OK with me,' Ruby said.

'We can have it at my house tomorrow, if you can get a lift over,' Laura said. 'You could get your mum to drop you over after ballet, Ruby.'

'I'm sure Mum would give Hannah and me a lift,' I said. 'She can go over and visit Sadie and Grandad while we're rehearsing.'

Sadie and Grandad live across the road from Laura, which had come in handy a couple of times already.

'Cool,' said Hannah. 'Tomorrow it is then!'

Chapter Eleven

I was expecting the usual pandemonium when I rang Hannah's doorbell on Saturday morning, but her dad Steve answered, dressed in his gardening clothes.

'Oh, hi, Meg,' he said, smiling. 'I think Hannah's nearly ready.' He called up the stairs, 'Hannah!'

Hannah came running downstairs. 'Hi, Meg! I'll just grab my notebook. I've written down a few more ideas for the scenes.'

'Great,' I said. 'Me too!'

'So what's this latest show you're doing? Sleeping Beauty is it?' Hannah's dad said. 'Oh no, wait, that's just what we call Hannah when she can't get out of bed on Saturday mornings.'

'Daa-aad!' groaned Hannah. 'No dad jokes today please!'

'Of course not,' Steve said, winking at me. 'Do you need a lift home later, Sleeping ... I mean, Hannah?'

'No, we're fine thanks,' I said, seeing that Hannah was

merely looking thunderously at him. 'My mum is going to visit my grandparents while we're rehearsing, so she can bring us home too.'

'Ah, the famous acting dynasty!' Steve said. 'No wonder you've got the acting bug, Meg. I've no idea where Hannah gets her interest in it from. The nearest anyone in my family ever got to appearing on stage was when I was asked to come up to pick out a raffle ticket at the office Christmas dinner.'

Hannah, who had started blushing at Steve's mentioning the acting dynasty, now looked positively mortified. 'Dad, please! Come on, Meg, let's get out of here before Dad embarrasses me any more.'

'But it's my job to embarrass you!' Steve called after her as we made our escape. 'It's in the dad handbook!'

'Sorry about that,' Hannah muttered.

Strangely, I found myself feeling a tiny bit envious of her easy relationship with her dad, and her crazy, action-packed family. I wished my dad could be around a bit more – and would pay a bit more attention to us when he was. At least Steve knew what Hannah was up to, and I was pretty sure he'd got the show wrong on purpose. My dad only seemed to want to talk about his film.

Mum was waiting for us in the car. 'All set?' she asked as I slipped into the front seat beside her and Hannah got in at the back. 'I hear you two are going to be the ugly stepsisters, Hannah. It's going to be quite a task to pull that one off!'

'Oh, we'll have great fun with the costumes and make-up!' Hannah said. 'You won't know us when we've finished!'

'I'm sure you're right, darling,' Mum said. 'I played the Wicked Witch of the West once, you know, from *The Wizard of Oz*? What a palaver that was, good heavens! I used to need to spend a whole hour getting my face done each night. I was quite relieved when that show came to an end.'

'I don't remember hearing about that one before, Mum,' I said, surprised.

'Well, it's not exactly the type of photo you want to hang up in your house, darling!' Mum said with a laugh. 'Green never was my colour!'

She started telling Hannah all about different productions she'd appeared in over the years which had required specialist make-up. In the rearview mirror, I could see that Hannah was absolutely riveted, though all she kept saying was 'Wow' or 'Really?' Just the kind of attentive audience my mum likes, I thought with a smile to myself. Sometimes it took this sort of encounter to remind me how unusual my upbringing really was. Not everyone had a mother who'd once had such a severe allergic reaction to greasepaint that she couldn't leave the house for a week.

'Oh, it was simply ghastly, wasn't it Meg?' Mum said, shuddering at the memory. 'My face was covered in the most dreadful blisters. Doug had to do all the shopping – I think it was the first time he discovered where the supermarket was! But this is how we actresses must suffer for our art.'

'Mum, you'll scare Hannah!' I said, though from the look on Hannah's face she seemed quite prepared to suffer for her art if that was necessary. 'We're only going to be using ordinary make-up so I think we'll be OK.'

'I suppose you don't have to worry about stage lighting if you're going to be outdoors again,' Mum said. 'That's why you need the really strong greasepaint, you know, Hannah – because under stage lighting even the best tans look terribly pale! Are you planning another garden show?'

'We haven't really talked about that yet,' I said. 'I guess we could do it in the garden again, but it might have to be pretty soon before the weather gets cold.'

'Let's talk about it today,' Hannah said, writing it down in her notebook.

'Well, here we are!' Mum said, pulling up outside Sadie's house. 'Have a fun rehearsal girls, and see you back here at one.'

Ruby was just arriving at Laura's too. Laura was already at the front door ready to let us in. 'I can't wait to get started!' she said. 'I've got loads of ideas for scenes.'

'So have I,' Hannah, Ruby and I said at exactly the same time. This was the perfect cue for a fit of giggles, which caused Laura's big sister Andrea to roll her eyes at us as she passed by on her way up to her room with her friend Maeve.

'Oh no, it's the giggle gang again,' she said to Maeve. 'Cover your ears, they think everything's hilarious.'

'Have fun studying,' Laura responded at once. 'Glad I don't have to do homework on the weekend.' She turned to us before Andrea could reply. 'Come on guys, let's go out to the garden.'

Gardens seemed to have become our ideal rehearsal space, but already there was a feel of autumn in the air, and I realised we'd have to start thinking about a plan for when it got too cold to rehearse outside. Of course we could use someone's sitting room or bedroom, but it had been great having all the space outdoors. Then there was the show itself – we'd definitely need more space than any of our sitting rooms if we had to accommodate an audience too.

One by one we climbed into Laura's trampoline which is our favourite place to sit in our garden. It's very relaxing sitting there chatting and having a gentle bounce every now and again.

'Let's get the official business out of the way first,' Hannah said. 'We should make a plan about when we're going to do the show – and where.'

'Yes, you're right, it really helped us to focus last time,' Laura said. 'Maybe we could do it in school?'

'Do you think Miss Brennan would let us?' I asked. 'It would be nice to do it for the class.'

'I'm sure she would,' Ruby said. 'She seems really nice so far, doesn't she?'

'Yes – apart from all the maths homework,' Hannah said. 'I think school sounds like a good plan, especially because – well, I'll get to that idea in a minute. What about rehearsals? It's soon going to be too cold to use our gardens.'

'Oh, we might have a few more weeks,' Laura said. 'It's lovely today.'

'That's true,' Hannah said. 'It's actually quite warm when the sun comes out! OK, maybe we don't need to worry about it just yet. So what about a date? Do you think we'd be ready by the end of September?'

'I think so,' I said. 'As long as we can fit in at least three rehearsals a week.'

'I'm not sure I'll be able to do three every week,' Ruby said. 'My ballet teacher is talking about doing some extra rehearsals for our Christmas show.'

'You're already doing three classes a week, isn't that enough?' Laura complained.

'Well, what about you with all your Gaelic football training and matches?' Ruby flashed back. I'd noticed that those two seemed to be getting on each other's nerves a little bit recently, and that Laura especially didn't seem to have much patience for Ruby's ballet obsession.

'I'm sure we can work around everyone's timetable,' Hannah said, trying to smooth things over. 'Maybe we could fit in short rehearsals at lunch time in school or something.'

'Can we get started on the show itself then?' I asked. I was dying to get on with trying out my stepsister act.

'Yes please!' Hannah said. 'Let's hear some of these brilliant ideas! Who wants to go first?'

'I will,' said Laura. 'How about we start off with the ugly stepsisters making Cinderella do their homework for them? That's pretty modern.'

'Why does Cinderella just do what they say, though?' Ruby said. 'I've been wondering about that.'

'How about they keep threatening to tell their mother on her?' I suggested. I put on a whiny, bossy voice. 'Cinderella, get that maths done right now or I'm going to tell Mummy you were mean to me – Cinderella, make me a snack or I'll tell Mummy you broke her vase!'

Ruby was giggling. 'That sounds great. Oh, maybe the stepsisters could actually break a vase on stage and then act like it was Cinderella who did it.'

'I wonder if my mum has any of her old pottery left,' I said. 'There might be some in Sadie's attic. She wouldn't mind us smashing those!'

'I had an idea for the cool auntie,' Laura said. 'How about she's a good witch? You know, she's an ordinary auntie by day, works in an office, but she's secretly a witch.'

'But I thought she was going to give Cinderella a make-over instead of using magic,' I said.

'Oh yes, I'd forgotten about that,' Laura said, disappointed.

'We could do a witch show for Hallowe'en and do something like that then,' Hannah suggested. 'That would be so much fun! But getting back to Cinderella – I was thinking, how about she's going to the sixth class graduation disco?'

'Oh, yes!' exclaimed Ruby and Laura together.

I'd already heard so much about the sixth class graduation disco, even though it wouldn't be happening until the end of the school year in June. It seemed to be a pretty big deal in our school. Sixth class was the last year of primary school – afterwards we'd be moving on to secondary school and the class would be all split up. So the graduation ceremony and the disco that followed were almost like a rite of passage.

We talked about all our different ideas. Hannah's pen flew over the pages of her notebook as she scribbled everything down. In the end, we'd managed to come up with what we thought was a pretty clever plot.

Cindy (which we thought was more suited to our show

than Cinderella) was being bullied by her two stepsisters, who made her do all their homework, clean their rooms and bring them snacks and drinks. (We'd made the stepsisters twins, the same age as Cindy, so they could all be in the same class in school, which suited our story.) Cindy was longing to go to the graduation disco, but she had nothing to wear, because her only clothes were her stepsisters' old hand-me-downs which didn't fit her properly. She did her best to make herself an outfit, but the stepsisters ruined it. They went off to the disco without her and she was left alone in her room, crying. That was when her cool auntie arrived with a fabulous new outfit for her to wear, did her hair and make-up and gave her a lift to the disco.

At the disco Cindy met Disco Boy (which was what we were calling Prince Charming for now because we couldn't seem to agree on a name) who thought she was the most beautiful girl he'd ever seen. He danced with her all night and the stepsisters were so jealous. But Cindy lost one of her new Converse and ran home without it.

Next morning, Disco Boy found Cindy and gave her her shoe back. He asked her to marry him and come to live with him in his mansion. But Cindy said no thanks, because they were only twelve, and she was going to go and live with her cool aunt instead. The ugly stepsisters were very jealous that Disco Boy liked Cindy instead of them and even more jealous that Cindy got to live with the cool aunt, but it served them right for being so mean.

'How are we going to do the disco scene?' Hannah asked. 'Will it work with only four people?'

'Maybe the scene could be set at the soft drinks table, a little bit away from the main action,' I said. 'That would make sense anyway, because that's where people would go to chat at a disco – you can't really chat on the dance floor.'

'Yes, and we could have some sort of backdrop to make it look like there are more people there,' Hannah said, excited. 'Maybe we could hang up an old sheet and paint some figures on it – you know, just black silhouettes.'

'I have a disco ball we could use,' Ruby exclaimed. 'We just need to be able to plug it in somewhere and then it will send coloured lights all around the stage. That would help make it look like the silhouettes were other people at the disco.'

'That sounds great,' Hannah said. 'And we'd need some music of course. I guess if the music's not too loud that will help give the impression that the disco is sort of in the background.'

'Great, let's get started then,' said Laura. 'Should we start at the beginning?'

We started improvising the first scene with the ugly stepsisters and Cindy. Laura wasn't in that scene so she took notes for us. I loved that I was finally getting the chance to practise the snooty looks and nasty comments I had in mind for my part.

We were so absorbed in our acting that we didn't realise Andrea and Maeve had snuck out to the garden to watch us until a smothered giggle gave them away. Laura turned around, outraged.

'Andrea! Go away or I'm telling Mum. She told you to leave us alone.'

'Oh, don't make us go away!' Andrea begged. 'It's really funny.'

'The stepsisters are brilliant,' Maeve chimed in.

Laura was about to argue, but Hannah, who loves any kind of constructive criticism, got in before her. 'Do you really think so?' she asked. 'Did you see the bit where I threw Cindy's favourite necklace out the window?'

'Yes, it was great,' Andrea said.

'You guys are good!' Maeve said. 'You could be the next Saoirse Ronan or Daisy Sheridan!'

I felt all the colour drain out of my face. How could Maeve possibly know that name?

'Who's Daisy Sheridan?' Hannah asked.

'Haven't you heard of her? She's this young Irish actress, about your age I think,' Maeve explained. 'She's supposed to be something special. Her first film is coming out soon – I forget what it's called.'

'Oh, we'll have to go and see that,' Hannah said, excited.

'Imagine someone our age – and from Ireland. Maybe your dad knows her, Meg.'

I tried to laugh. 'My dad doesn't, like, know everyone in all the films …' I gripped my hands tightly to stop them shaking and did my best to sound casual as I asked, 'Where did you hear about her, anyway?'

'Oh I follow all the celebrity gossip on Twitter,' Maeve said. 'I saw it on there.'

'Oh, right.' I turned to my friends. 'Well, will we get on with the scene?'

'After they go,' Laura said, frowning at Andrea and Maeve. 'We're not ready for an audience yet.'

'OK, we can take a hint!' Andrea said. 'Come on, Maeve, we should probably finish that maths anyway.'

We went back to our rehearsal, but the morning was kind of ruined for me. I tried to concentrate on my part, but it was hard not to be distracted by all sorts of panicky thoughts, whirling around my head.

* * *

When we got home I waited until Mum was busy before taking out the laptop. I quickly typed Daisy Sheridan into Google. Straight away a story popped up, written by someone calling herself Tinseltown Talk: 'Young Irish starlet Daisy Sheridan, soon to appear in a major motion picture, is set to be the next big sensation. With all the quiet charm of Saoirse Ronan and the charisma of Evanna Lynch, Sheridan will wow audiences all over the world in her new role.'

Overcome with tension, I kept scrolling down, but this was the only story so far. I checked for a photo and heaved a sigh of relief that there didn't seem to be one. At least that was something.

But why was the story there at all? This wasn't supposed to happen for ages yet.

'Doing some more research for your show?'

I'd been so engrossed in the story I hadn't heard Mum come in. I instantly shut down Google, turning to smile at Mum. 'Yes, just thinking about costumes,' I said. 'I'm going to leave it now though. Is it time for lunch?'

'Yes, I'm just going to heat up some soup,' Mum said. 'Could you put the laptop away and set the table for me, there's a dear.'

I put the laptop away, glad Mum hadn't seen what I'd been reading. One thing was for sure, I was going to have to keep this to myself for now. Mum would absolutely go ballistic when she found out. Because there was only one person who could have released the story this early.

Chapter Twelve

I was finding it hard to get used to sitting in the classroom for six hours every day. It was so different from what I was used to, with all the chaos and bustle of being on the film set in between lessons. Here the only breaks were when we went outside to play at break time or for P.E. Even being sent to another class on a message was great because of the change of scene.

Stuck at my desk, my mind wandered a lot, especially when we were doing a subject I wasn't very interested in. Monday seemed to be the slowest day of all. Gazing out the window, I watched the leaves on the sycamore tree blowing in the autumn wind. Already they were starting to turn brown. Summer was well and truly over.

Suddenly I found my attention caught by something Miss Brennan was saying. 'Now, we have a special date coming up in a few weeks' time. Carrickbeg National School will be a hundred years old, and we have a big day of celebrations planned. All your families will be invited along to the School Centenary, and the Lord Mayor has promised to attend. We'll be decorating the school and baking cakes and so on. But here's the part that I know will really interest some of you. Fifth and sixth class have been asked to provide the entertainment. We're going to do a few songs together as a class, but we'll also have a drama section.'

I sat up straighter in my seat. Drama at school – excellent! I couldn't wait to hear what Miss Brennan had in mind.

'Now, the staff have decided that this is a project you should work on yourselves. So I want you to get into small groups of two to four and come up with a sketch together. It doesn't have to be very long – about five minutes is fine – and it can be based on a story or film or you can write something original yourselves. We're not going to do this in class time – I want it to be all your own work – and it will be a nice surprise for the rest of the class to see what you've come up with. Next week we will have a performance just for the class, and I'll choose a group to represent us at the celebration day concert.'

Hannah turned around in her seat to smile at me and I gave her the thumbs up in return. Our Cinderella show would be perfect for this! And now we'd have a brilliant excuse to get together more often because it was homework. Laura and Ruby were whispering together and I knew they'd had the same idea.

Miss Brennan was still talking. 'So it might be easier to choose someone who lives near you so you can get together to work on it. I don't want to create a lot of work for your parents in setting up play dates!'

Tracey put her hand on my arm. 'Great! We can work on this together. What do you think we should do?'

'Oh – um …' I didn't know what to say. I couldn't very well tell her that I'd already agreed to work with Star Club, when the other three were sitting all the way at the front of the classroom.

'Don't worry, I'm sure I can come up with something, I have loads of great ideas,' Tracey said. 'Oh, how about we make a music video?'

'Uh, I'm not sure that's what Miss Brennan means …' I began.

'No, you're right. She probably wants something a bit more traditional. Well, how about we're two sisters who want to be pop stars, and we're fighting because we both think we're better than the other? Or how about we're judges on *X Factor*, and we can be really nasty and mock all the contestants?'

In spite of myself I found I was nodding along to Tracey's ideas, though she was talking so much I didn't actually say anything. She finally paused to take a breath before saying,

'Why don't you come over to my house after school and we can get started?'

'I can't today,' I said, glad to have a good excuse. 'My granny collects me on Mondays and we go back to hers.'

'Oh. Well, never mind, we can do it another day. It's so handy us living so close! We'll be able to get together every day if we want to.'

'All right, boys and girls, I know you're excited, but let's move on now,' Miss Brennan said. 'Take out your Spellbound books please.'

Tracey sighed dramatically and made a big show of searching through her bag. I opened my book, a tense feeling in the pit of my stomach. How was I going to get out of this one?

* * *

Our Star Club meeting that afternoon was in Hannah's again. It was really my turn to be the host, but Mum wouldn't be home by 5pm so I couldn't have people over. Mum was happy to let me stay home on my own, but she knew some of the other mums wouldn't be happy to have their kids visit without an adult present. I'd promised to host on Friday instead, when Mum got off earlier.

I was the first one there and Hannah answered the door, full of excitement. 'Hi, Meg! I was looking for you after school, but you must have gone straight off with Sadie. Isn't it cool about the drama project for the School Centenary? I've already told Mum we're going to need extra rehearsal time because it's homework!'

'Cool,' I said, squashing down the uncomfortable thought that Tracey was expecting me to do the project with her. 'I wish all homework could be like that!'

'Come up to my room,' Hannah said. 'It's a bit too chilly for the garden this evening, so I've bribed Maisie to stay away for an hour. I have to play Maisie Monopoly with her later, but it's a small price to pay for a bit of peace and quiet.'

'Maisie Monopoly' is what Hannah calls Maisie's version of the game, because Maisie has pretty much made up her own rules. I played it with all the Kielys one day during the holidays. It went on for four hours and Maisie, inevitably, won, mainly because the rest of us got so confused by the rules that we eventually just started letting her buy all our property at knock-down prices. I thought it was pretty self-sacrificing of Hannah to agree to a game just so we could have our rehearsal. I wondered, though, if we'd have enough room in her bedroom – I'd been up there before, and with the twin beds belonging to Hannah and Maisie there wasn't room for much else.

Hannah led the way up to her room, where she opened the door with a flourish. 'Ta-da!' she said, letting me go in first.

'Oh wow, you got bunks!' I said, admiring the lovely bunk beds with their matching duvet covers, yellow with purple and pink butterflies.

'Great, isn't it?' Hannah said, beaming. 'We have so much more space now. It used to drive me crazy trying to walk around our beds when I was practising my lines. We didn't even need new beds – the ones we had could be either bunk beds or twin – Dad just didn't want to put them up as bunks before because he thought Maisie would dive-bomb off the top bunk, but she's promised to behave.'

'It's brilliant – you must be thrilled,' I said.

'I'd still prefer to have my own room, but looks like I'll have to wait a bit longer for that,' Hannah said.

The doorbell rang and Ruby and Laura came running up the stairs to join us, exclaiming in delight when they saw Hannah's revamped room. It was amazing how much difference it made to the bedroom – it would definitely work much better as a rehearsal space.

'Let's get started then, will we?' Hannah said. 'Oh, and we still need names for the characters – apart from Cindy of course. Anyone come up with anything?'

'How about Faye for the fairy godmother?' Laura said. 'It means fairy, but it sounds like a normal name, so I think it would work.'

'Perfect!' Hannah said.

'We need something horrible for the ugly stepsisters,' I said. 'And matching – like maybe starting with the same letter, or rhyming or something. Like Prudence and Prunella.'

'Beryl and Cheryl,' said Laura.

'Mildred and Hildred,' said Ruby.

'Vienetta and Verucca,' Hannah said, giggling as she wrote all the suggestions down.

In the end we decided that I would be Hepzibah and Hannah would be Hortense, which we thought sounded just perfect for the kind of characters we were creating.

'What about Disco Boy?' Ruby asked. 'We haven't got a name for him yet.'

'Never mind, we haven't finished his scenes yet so we can leave him for now,' Hannah said. 'I'm dying to get started. Let's start with the bit where the stepsisters deliberately knock over the soup and make Cindy clean it up.'

We had the best time bringing the stepsisters to life. I noticed, though, that Ruby was a bit unsure in her role as Cinderella, and Laura kept getting impatient with her when she didn't know her lines.

'Don't worry, Ruby,' I said, trying to smooth things over. 'It's still really early in our rehearsals.'

'I think we're all probably hungry too!' Hannah said. 'Laura, why don't you come with me and help me get a snack ready?'

Laura got up to help, and as they were leaving Hannah whispered to me, 'See if you can give Ruby a hand.'

Ruby was walking around with the script in her hand, feverishly going over her lines.

'Want me to go over that bit with you, Ruby?' I asked tentatively.

'It's too hard,' Ruby burst out. 'I did *say* I didn't think I should be Cinderella. There are too many lines for me.' She looked almost tearful.

'But you're a fabulous Cinderella,' I told her. 'I think maybe we just need to make the part suit you better. What about if we cut out a few lines? I'm sure she doesn't need to say so much.' I took the script, where Ruby had high-lighted her own lines in pink. There really was quite a lot for her to learn. 'Look, that bit can come out, it's not important to the story,' I said, pointing. 'And we can make that line much shorter. And that bit can come out too. You don't need to say so many words – you can use body language to show how you feel when you're being bullied by your stepsisters.'

Ruby nodded, but she didn't look completely con-vinced. 'I don't know, Meg. I just don't know if I'm right for the part. It's not like Posy, which felt like a natural fit to me, with the ballet and everything.'

I had a flash of inspiration. 'But we can have dancing in this too. Why don't we put in a dance for Cinderella in the disco scene?'

'Oh, could we?' Ruby said, her face lighting up. 'That would be fantastic. I think I could do a much better job of getting the character across if I could use movement. I could choreograph something that shows how Cinderella feels so happy to be at the disco, and free from the mean stepsisters.' She started moving gracefully around the room in a floaty, dreamy sort of dance, swaying in time to some music only she could hear.

'That would be perfect,' I told her. I wondered if Hannah would mind me changing things around. It was really the director's job to make the sort of changes I was suggesting, but then again it had always been a team effort for us in planning our show. Even though Hannah could be bossy at times, she was nothing like some directors I'd seen before, who were almost like dictators on set.

Hannah and Laura came back with a plateful of carrot sticks and houmous. Hannah was delighted when I told her what Ruby and I had come up with.

'That sounds fantastic, guys!' she said. 'I love the idea of using dance to show how Cindy is feeling!'

'Sorry I was grumpy,' Laura added a bit sheepishly. 'I think Hannah was right, I just needed to get some food into me. Even if it's just carrots.'

'That was all Mum would let us have this close to

dinner time,' Hannah explained. 'You know what she's like!'

'It's perfect,' I told her, grabbing a handful of carrots. 'Ruby, why don't you show them the dance you were doing? I think this is really going to work.'

Chapter Thirteen

At home, I had just sat down and switched on the TV, thinking I'd chill out for a few minutes, when I heard Mum's key in the front door. She came storming into the sitting room and flung her jacket on the back of the couch any old way. I watched as it slid onto the floor. Mum didn't bother picking it up, just flung herself onto the couch instead.

'Bad day at work?' I asked sympathetically.

'You could say that, darling,' Mum said, sighing theatrically.

'Is it that computer program again? Or Chris?' I asked. Chris was Mum's boss in the office where she worked.

'Neither. The program's going just fine now, and Chris thinks I'm fabulous. It's your dad!'

My heart sank. 'What's he done this time?'

Mum sighed again. 'What *hasn't* he done? He keeps emailing me and texting me promotional photos from the new film, asking me to choose one, and when I ignored his call on my mobile he rang the office. Honestly, darling, doesn't he understand that I'm in work? I can't keep dropping everything to answer his silly questions.'

'Why is he in such a rush with the photos?' I asked, trying to fight a sense of foreboding. I wondered if Mum had seen the 'Tinseltown Talk' story. Probably not, I decided, or she'd be even angrier.

'I really can't imagine,' Mum said. 'The film isn't due out for months! I simply can't see what the panic is. And then he starts up again about wanting you to go back out to California. Can't he accept we just want a quiet life for a little while?'

Mum looked exhausted by the stress of it all. I went and sat beside her, giving her a clumsy one-armed hug.

'Do you want me to talk to him?' I asked. 'Maybe he would listen to me.' I didn't really think that he would, but I badly wanted to try to make Mum feel better.

But Mum shook her head emphatically. 'Absolutely not. I'm not having you used as a pawn between us.'

'I know you wouldn't,' I said, though for a moment I wondered. Sometimes my parents acted like couples are supposed to act when they're getting divorced – using the children for information and to pass on messages, trying to win them over to their own side. Surely though my parents weren't going to get divorced? They were always fighting like this – and then they'd make it up again and be so lovey-dovey with each other that it was absolutely sickening. I'd always figured this was just the way it was when you had two such highly-strung artistic temperaments coming up against each other. Sometimes I thought I was the sanest one of the three of us.

'Let's put it out of our heads,' Mum said. 'I don't much feel like cooking dinner after the day I've had. Let's see what's in the freezer, will we? There should still be some of Sadie's casserole left. I knew that would come in handy.'

* * *

Next day in school, Tracey kept whispering to me in class about what she thought we should do for the School Centenary show.

'I hope you don't mind, but Jamie and I got started without you,' she whispered. 'We're going to be the two *X Factor* judges and you can be the pop star who we think is rubbish.'

'Uh, Tracey …'

'You can do some really terrible singing, right? Something awful and screechy, and we'll make fun of you and then you get thrown off the show.'

It didn't sound like a whole lot of fun for the poor pop star, I thought. At least Cinderella had a happy ending.

'I'm just not sure ...' I started.

'Enough talking, you two!' Miss Brennan interrupted. 'Get on with your work please!'

I turned my attention back to my work, glad of the interruption. I knew I needed to tell Tracey I wasn't going to do it, but she was so forceful, it was hard to find the right words.

Chapter Fourteen

It was lovely being able to walk to school with Hannah and Ruby every morning. I'd given up calling for Tracey, who always seemed to leave earlier. I didn't know why she was avoiding us – she was still very friendly to me in class. And she was still convinced we were going to work together on the sketch for the School Centenary. So far I'd avoided actually committing to something – but I hadn't told her I was doing it with Star Club.

That Friday when we got to the school yard, something felt different. Kids fell silent as we went past, then immediately started whispering among themselves. Some of the boys even stopped kicking a ball around to turn and stare at us as we went by. Or to stare at me.

'Oh my God, Meg! Is it true?' Isabel was actually jumping up and down with excitement, and even Sean and Aaron, who normally pretend to be too cool to be interested in anything girls have to say, edged in close to us, eager to hear my reply.

'Is what true?' I asked, though I had a sinking feeling I knew exactly what she was talking about.

'That your parents work in films!' Isabel said, almost breathless with excitement.

Beside me, I heard a sharp intake of breath from Hannah. Isabel carried on, 'Everyone's talking about it. They're saying your mum's an actress and your dad's a director. Is it true?'

I could almost feel thousands of eyes on me, waiting for me to say something. Dimly, I realised that the way I reacted now could determine my whole future at Carrick-beg National School – in fact, in Carrickbeg itself. I swallowed. 'Yes, it's true. But they're not, like, madly famous or anything. I mean, it's not like they're involved in the *Harry Potter* films or something.' I tried to laugh. 'My mum has been in a few films, but she mainly works in the theatre. And my dad mainly works in TV – the film he's working on now is his first mainstream one.'

'But he's actually working in Hollywood, right?' Isabel asked, wide-eyed.

'Uh – yes,' I admitted.

'Oh my God, I can't believe it!' Isabel squealed. 'Aoife, it's true!'

It looked like my attempt to play it down hadn't exactly worked. Hannah and Ruby looked as dismayed as I felt.

Isabel was waving frantically to Aoife, who left her place at the top of the line and ran down to join us. Within seconds we were surrounded by what seemed like the whole of sixth class, with a couple of extra kids from fourth and fifth class trying to see what was going on too. Only Tracey stayed in her place, not looking at us, her attention fixed firmly on her phone.

Everyone was firing questions at me at once.

'What films is your mum in?'

'What's her name? Would we have heard of her?'

'Why did you move to Carrickbeg? Why aren't you in Hollywood with your dad?'

'What's it like in Hollywood?'

'Are your parents millionaires?'

It was even worse than I'd imagined. Surrounded by all these kids, all shouting over each other, all staring at me, I felt panic-stricken and completely alone. Then I felt the comforting touch of Hannah's hand on my arm, and on the other side Ruby pressed closer to me too.

The bell rang, but kids took absolutely no notice, crowding around me even closer until I felt completely hemmed in.

Hannah took charge. Sometimes her bossy big sister thing is an absolute blessing. 'OK guys, calm down, it's not like Niall Horan just walked into the yard.'

'Oh my God, do you know Niall Horan?' cried Aoife.

'Of course she doesn't!' Hannah said.

'What's going on here?' It was Miss Brennan, sounding distinctly unimpressed at finding her class in a hysterical huddle instead of a neat line. The kids from fourth and fifth class melted away, running after their own class lines which were already on their way into the school.

'Oh, Miss!' Isabel was so excited she didn't even notice how cross Miss Brennan looked. 'Meg's parents are famous! They're in films! Meg used to live in Hollywood!'

Miss Brennan's expression didn't change. 'That's very nice I'm sure, but that doesn't explain why my class are out in the yard five minutes after the bell has gone. Please try to remember you're the oldest class in the school and we expect you to set a good example to the younger children. What would the junior infants think if they saw sixth class swarming around like a colony of demented wasps instead of lining up neatly?'

'Sorry, Miss,' Isabel murmured, moving swiftly back into her place.

Miss Brennan waited until everyone had lined up behind Tracey, who still hadn't moved, then she marched to the head of the line herself to lead us into the class-room.

I wondered for a minute why she hadn't shown any reaction to what Isabel had told her. Maybe she thought Isabel was making it up? But then it hit me that Mum must have told the school so they would be prepared for something like this. Although none of us could have expected it to happen so soon.

How had it got out? Surely none of my Star Club friends had said anything, not after me reminding them again. Not after me being so cross when Hannah had almost given it away on the first day. But then I remembered how she had let it slip without meaning to – maybe something like that had happened again?

I tried to calm myself down, taking some deep breaths as we walked down the corridor. Hannah and Ruby, ignoring the rule about walking in single file, were still closely pressed on either side of me. I found their presence both comforting and worrying. Could I really trust them, or was it one of them who had let me down?

When we got to the classroom I sank into my seat, trying not to catch anyone's eye. Beside me, Tracey's gaze was fixed firmly on the front of the classroom.

'All right class, I think we'll skip news today and go straight to maths,' Miss Brennan said, calmly ignoring the groans that followed this. 'Take out your homework please and we'll see how you got on.'

Tracey waited until Miss Brennan's back was turned as she began working out some of the sums on the whiteboard. Then she whispered, 'So it is true then.'

I didn't bother going through with the charade of asking

what she meant. 'Yes,' I said quietly.

She turned to me with a look of deep hurt in her eyes. 'But you said it was all a joke about Hollywood.'

'I'm sorry,' I said. 'I wanted to tell you, but Mum insisted we keep it a secret.'

'I felt like an idiot this morning when Isabel asked me if it was true,' Tracey said in a small, sad voice. 'I said, "Of course it's not true because Meg and I are such good friends, she would never have lied to me."'

'I know, Tracey. I'm really sorry …'

'I told Isabel, "I've gone out of my way to be kind to Meg since she moved in, and even though for some reason she doesn't want to walk to school with me I've kept trying to be as helpful as I can. I've refused to listen to Hannah when she was saying nasty things about Meg, because she's my friend."'

'Tracey …'

'I wish you could have trusted me, Meg,' she went on quietly. 'I'd never blab someone's secrets to the whole class like other people do. I wouldn't have told anyone if you asked me not to. I thought we were friends.'

'We are,' I said lamely.

'I hope so,' Tracey said, her tone suddenly lighter again. 'I can see that you really need a friend right now, because the people you thought you could trust – Hannah and the others – have let you down, haven't they? Telling everyone your secret?'

I said nothing. I didn't know what to think any more.

Chapter Fifteen

At break time, the second Miss Brennan said we could go outside, I bolted for the door before anyone else had even left their seat. I raced down the corridor, completely ignoring the rule about no running indoors. I had to get outside before anyone else could see where I was going.

Our school has three different yards – one for the three youngest classes, one for the three middle classes, and the smallest one for the two oldest classes. But I didn't go to the fifth and sixth class yard as usual. I'd seen something in the junior yard that I'd meant to explore – a little gap in the hedge that made me think of the secret passage into Hannah's garden. I didn't know if it led anywhere, but this seemed like a good time to find out.

I reached the hedge just before the first of the junior and senior infants got into their yard and squeezed my way through. It was a lot tighter than the way into Hannah's garden, which had gotten wider with all our trips back and forth. But that meant no one else had been through here recently, which was just what I wanted.

On the other side of the hedge was the high wall that surrounded the school – and that was it. Just a narrow space in between – no magic door to the other side, no secret garden to escape to. But if I'd timed it right, and I was pretty sure that I had, then no one knew I was here. And that was all I needed.

An old packing crate, probably thrown in behind the hedge after some school fête and then forgotten about, made a seat. Not very comfortable, but it would do. Safe at last from all those prying eyes that I'd felt watching me in the classroom all morning, I felt the tears starting to flow down my cheeks. Sitting down, I took out Sadie's locket and let the chain run through my fingers, pretending she was beside me to make me feel better.

The yard was filling up with kids now, the shouts and cries sounding slightly muffled through the hedge, games of catch being started and clamouring to other kids to join in. I stayed where I was, the hedge a solid green barrier between the real world and me.

'Meg!' That sounded like Ruby's voice. Was she in the junior yard? How did they know I was here? I didn't answer. I wrapped my arms around myself, trying to get warm. In my rush I hadn't brought my jacket and it was starting to feel a bit chilly.

'Meg, where are you? Meg!'

Now it was Hannah. I stayed quiet. They couldn't know where I was – maybe they would give up and go away. I didn't want to talk to anyone.

Suddenly Laura's head appeared through the hedge right beside me. I gasped in fright.

'You guys, she's here!' Laura squeezed herself in and sat down beside me, putting her arm around me.

Next moment, Ruby appeared, and by the time Hannah had squished in too the space felt narrower than ever.

In spite of myself, I laughed. 'Well, this is cosy,' I said. 'So much for finding a top secret hideaway. How did you find me?'

'We knew you wouldn't have left the school, so we just kept looking,' Laura said. 'Then I saw the gap in the hedge.'

'I hope no one else followed you,' I said.

'No, I don't think so, it's only the small kids out there,' Hannah said. 'Meg, are you OK? We're worried about you.'

'I don't know,' I said. 'I just don't want to deal with all this. I can't face the attention.'

'It'll all be forgotten soon,' Laura said. 'It's just one of those things, everyone's so excited today, but in a few days they'll have moved on to something else.'

'Do you really think so?' I asked, trying to wipe away my tears with my sleeve. Hannah fished around in her pocket and found me a tissue which I gratefully accepted.

'Definitely,' Hannah said. 'It's like when Aaron won a trip to see an Ireland match and the whole class was talking about it, but by the next day it was old news.'

I sniffed and wiped my nose with the tissue. No one said anything for a minute. Then I said, quietly but feeling determined to ask, 'How do you think people found out, anyway? You guys didn't say anything?'

'No, of course we didn't,' Ruby said at once. 'We promised we wouldn't, Meg, and we didn't.'

She looked around at the other two, who were shaking their heads vigorously. Hannah was blushing again but she said, 'I swear I didn't, Meg. I've been *so* careful ever since I made that mistake on the first day of school. I even warned my parents not to say anything – that's why I was so embarrassed when my dad started going on about the acting dynasty the other day.'

'Oh, that.' I thought back to what Hannah's dad had said when I called for her. I'd been too busy feeling jealous of how interested he was in our show to really take much notice of what he'd said about my family.

'It's probably just one of those small town things, Meg,' Laura said. 'People must know your granny and grandad, and maybe they even saw your mum in the theatre when she used to live in Ireland, before you came back this time I mean. You couldn't have kept it a secret forever in a place like Carrickbeg.'

'That's true,' I admitted. 'I just thought with having a different surname from my mum's family people mightn't make the connection right away. Howard is my dad's surname, of course, and he's not famous. Not yet anyway!'

'We're just going to have to tell people to stop making morons of themselves,' Hannah said decisively. 'Flocking around you like you're some kind of superstar! It's ridiculous.'

'Or maybe you should just try to get used to it!' Laura said. 'I mean, when Star Club gets famous, we're all going to be surrounded by reporters every time we walk out the door! We'll be like that Daisy person Maeve was talking about.'

'That's right,' Ruby giggled. 'We'll have to have our hair and make-up done just to pop down to the shops.'

'Yes, and everyone's going to want to get our autographs, and take selfies with us,' Hannah said. 'We should really start practising our poses now. Which do you think is my best angle?'

The girls started messing around, posing in different positions, and making me laugh. I felt bad for even thinking one of them could have told people about my parents when they'd promised not to. Laura was probably right – it was just a small town thing.

All of a sudden I realised that everything had gone quiet in the yard outside the hedge. I parted a few branches and peeped out. The yard was empty!

'We must have missed the bell,' I said. 'I'm so sorry, I'll have got you all in trouble.'

'This was more important,' Laura said at once.

'I'm sure Miss Brennan will understand,' Hannah said.

Even Ruby, who hates getting into trouble, was nodding.

'We'd better go,' I said. 'Do I look like I've been crying?'

'No,' said Hannah and Ruby together, but Laura said, 'Yes' and then the other two admitted that yes I did a bit.

'You can splash your face with water when we get in,' Hannah said.

She led the way out. We ran as quickly as we could through the infant yard, not looking to see if anyone was watching us out the classroom windows. The others waited while I ducked into the bathroom to wash my face. I examined my eyes in the mirror. Still a bit red, but they'd have to do. I grabbed some toilet paper and stuffed it up my sleeve in case I needed it, then we hurried down the corridor to our classroom.

I waited for Miss Brennan to start scolding, prepared to take the blame and defend my three friends who were just looking after me. But to all of our surprise Miss Brennan just said, 'Into your places quickly, girls, and take out your history copies please. We're doing some brainstorming for our School Centenary projects.'

We didn't need to be told twice. I wondered what was going on. Did Miss Brennan realise I just needed to get away for a few minutes? I looked up at her as she passed by my desk, checking over everyone's work, and she gave me the tiniest wink.

* * *

After school, I was on my way out the side door with Hannah and Ruby when I realised I'd forgotten the book I needed for my project.

'I'd better go back and get it,' I said. 'Otherwise I won't be able to do my homework.'

'We'll wait for you,' Hannah said.

'No, you guys go on,' I told her, knowing Hannah's mum would want her home to help out.

I didn't wait for her to answer, turning quickly back towards our classroom. I knew Miss Brennan wouldn't be there, as she had headed towards the office after seeing us out, but the classroom would still be open because she'd asked Tracey and Jamie to stay behind and put away the art things. I should be able to grab my book quickly and maybe even catch up with the others.

Outside the classroom door, I caught the sound of voices. I was about to go in, but I stopped dead when I heard my own name.

'So you knew about Meg's family already then?' That was Jamie's voice.

'Of course,' Tracey said. 'Meg tells me everything.'

'But I thought I heard you saying you were upset she hadn't told you.'

Tracey laughed. 'No, you must have misunderstood. Of *course* I knew already. I've been over to Meg's house loads of times, and her mum is always so nice to me. She's not like you'd imagine a famous actress to be, you know? She's so friendly and down to earth. And her dad is great fun, always goofing around. They're so glad Meg and I are friends. They're planning on inviting me to their next film premiere. It would be nice company for Meg to have someone her own age there. That's what her mum said, anyway.'

'Wow, lucky you.' Jamie seemed to be hanging on her every word.

I couldn't believe what I was hearing. How could Tracey make up all that stuff? Why would she lie like that?

'Anyway, we'd better get going, that's everything done now,' Tracey said.

Not wanting her to know I'd overheard, I turned and ran. My project could wait. This was all just too weird.

Chapter Sixteen

I'd never been so glad it was Friday. It was such a relief to forget all about school for a while and just hang out with my Star Club friends. We all met up in my house to have another rehearsal.

Mum came out to the garden to bring us all some snacks. 'Here you go, darlings! I'm sure you must be absolutely starving. I know I always feel like I could eat an elephant after a tough rehearsal.'

'You know, your mum is really more like a cool auntie than a mum,' Laura said thoughtfully, after Mum had gone. 'I think I'm going to model Auntie Faye on her. You don't mind, do you, Meg?'

'No,' I said, laughing. 'This could be interesting!'

The rehearsal went well.

'That was good, wasn't it?' I said to Hannah as we were saying goodbye. 'I feel like it's starting to come together now.'

'Thank goodness, too,' Hannah said. 'Miss Brennan says she wants to see what we've done on Monday.'

'Did she? I didn't hear her. Maybe it was when she sent me out on a message,' I said, remembering that she'd given me a note to bring down to the secretary's office.

'It must have been,' Hannah said. 'I think she's going to choose the group to represent the class on Monday.'

'Really?' I asked, my stomach flipping over. This was it – I was just going to have to go over and tell Tracey now. Even if she was being weird, it wasn't fair to have her still planning her piece around me.

'Don't look so nervous!' Hannah said, misunderstanding my worry. 'We're doing really well now. I'm sure she's going to pick us!'

'Fingers crossed!' I said, forcing myself to smile.

I waited until they'd all gone, then, not wanting to give myself time to chicken out, I went straight over to Tracey's house and rang her doorbell.

Tracey opened the door, giving me one of her beaming smiles, which I noticed never seemed to quite reach her eyes. 'Meg! I was just talking to Jamie about the sketch earlier. We're really going to need to have a rehearsal with you as soon as possible!'

'I'm so sorry, Tracey,' I said, feeling worse than ever. 'I should have told you earlier. I said I'd do it with some of the other girls. Do you think you and Jamie can manage without me?'

Tracey's smile disappeared and for a moment quite a nasty look came into her eyes. But before I even had time to react she simply looked hurt, just like she had that morning. 'Well, I suppose we'll have to, won't we? I wish you'd told me sooner though – we were counting on you.'

'Sorry,' I said again. 'I know I should have.'

'Never mind,' Tracey said. 'I'm sure we'll get to do another project together. Well, I'd better go. Mum's just putting out dinner.'

'OK – have a nice weekend,' I said, but Tracey had already closed the door.

* * *

By Monday everyone seemed to be pretty much over the news about Mum and Dad. I did have a couple of kids from fourth class ask me if I knew Katy Perry, but that was about it.

Miss Brennan got everyone to do their sketches for the whole class. Everyone had chosen such different topics, it made for interesting viewing to see what they'd all come up with. Rilwan, whose family comes from Nigeria, had got some of his friends to do a sketch with him based on a Nigerian legend. They'd even got some traditional costumes – they looked fantastic. Sean played the guitar and he and his friends had put some music into their piece, which made it stand out. I didn't like Tracey and Jamie's piece very much, though. They did the *X Factor* sketch Tracey had been planning – they skipped the bit Tracey had wanted me to do, with the wannabe pop star singing really badly, and just went straight to the judges' comments. That could have worked fine, but they really didn't seem to have given the dialogue a lot of thought. I knew they thought they were being funny with all their mean comments about the singer, but it just came across as boring and repetitive. I felt a bit bad though – maybe if I'd joined in we could have made it better. Then I remembered all the mad things Tracey had told Jamie about me, and stopped feeling guilty.

Isabel and Aoife's sketch was especially good – they had chosen to act a piece about children coming to Carrickbeg National School when it first opened a hundred years ago. I was sure Miss Brennan would pick them because of the centenary theme – but I was wrong.

'Well, you were all absolutely wonderful, but we can only have one winner – or one group, I should say,' Miss Brennan said. 'The piece which will represent our class at the School Centenary next week is – *Cinderella*!'

The other Star Club girls and I looked at each other in delight. I couldn't believe it – we'd actually been picked! Led by Miss Brennan, the rest of the class started clapping.

Tracey kept her hands firmly in her lap, and I saw her whisper something to Jamie. But I was much too excited to worry about what Tracey thought.

* * *

That afternoon we were all a bit hyper when we met up at Hannah's house for our rehearsal. Hannah had a hard time getting us to concentrate.

'I can't believe it,' Ruby said, bouncing up and down. 'We've only been rehearsing for a couple of weeks!'

'We're naturals, that's why,' Laura said. 'Miss Brennan can recognise talent when she sees it!'

'Talent is one thing, but we definitely need more rehearsals,' Hannah said firmly. 'It's a huge responsibility representing the class! We'd better get stuck in.'

Unfortunately though, the rehearsal didn't go as well as the previous one. Ruby was too stiff in the role of Cindy – she complained that she felt too self-conscious. The step-sister lines didn't seem as funny as they had last time. And Laura was great at Auntie Faye, but she just wasn't convincing enough as Disco Boy – or Cameron as we were now calling him, after much debate.

'You know what would really help?' I said suddenly. 'If we could watch the movie. You know, the one with Lily James as Cinderella.'

'Oh, I love that one!' Ruby said. 'The costumes are fabulous!'

'I wonder if it's on Netflix,' Laura said.

'I've got the DVD,' I said. 'I can ask Mum if you can all come over and watch it. How about Friday? We could have our rehearsal at my house and watch the movie after.'

'That sounds great!' Hannah said. 'I've never seen it, I'd love to.'

'I'll ask Mum later,' I promised.

Chapter Seventeen

After dinner, over chocolate chip cookie ice cream, I told Mum the trouble we were having with our rehearsal and how I thought watching the film might help.

'That's a great idea,' Mum said. 'You can always learn so much from watching other actresses. When were you thinking of inviting the girls over?'

'Well, it's my turn to host our rehearsal on Friday,' I said. 'Could we maybe ask them to stay for pizza after the rehearsal and then watch the film?'

'I've got an even better idea,' Mum exclaimed. 'Why don't you invite them for a sleepover? You can have the whole evening together then, and watch the film in your pyjamas.'

Wow – this had gone even better than I could have hoped. 'Oh Mum, could we really? That would be brilliant!'

'Of course!' Mum said. 'It's a perfect opportunity. Just

as long as you promise you will get SOME sleep! I don't want three mothers on the phone to me on Saturday saying they're dealing with exhausted children who were awake all night! Not to mention me and the state I'd be in if I didn't get my beauty sleep!'

I laughed. 'Don't worry, Mum, I promise we'll get some sleep. A couple of hours anyway, once we finish telling ghost stories.'

Mum pretended to faint with horror. 'Well, I'll definitely be staying well away from those! I never did like ghost stories. They're all very well in the daylight – but at night, with the house dark and strange noises ...' She shuddered, then, the moment over, got up and started clearing our plates.

I couldn't wait to tell the girls about the sleepover plan. Then I realised that I didn't need to wait to tell Hannah at least. I ran out to the back garden and through the 'secret passage'.

Hannah was in the family room reading to Maisie. I knocked on the window and she looked up, smiling when she saw me. Maisie opened the window, looking less happy to see me. She fixed me with her famous 'Maisie stare', which despite her tiny size and cute blonde plaits is completely petrifying.

'Hannah's in the middle of reading me a book,' she informed me. 'So don't be too long, OK?'

'Maisie, don't be rude,' Hannah scolded, coming over to the window too.

'I won't be long, I just have to tell Hannah something quickly,' I promised Maisie. 'What book are you reading?'

'*Cinderella*,' Maisie said, showing me the cover. 'It's my favourite favourite.'

'Maisie is really looking forward to watching our Cinderella show, aren't you Maisie?' Hannah said, stressing the word 'watching'.

Maisie shrugged. 'I'll watch it,' she said, 'but I think it would be much more interesting if you had some animals in it. I was a very fantastic dog in my birthday show.'

'Of course you were,' I told her solemnly. 'It's just a pity we don't need any animals this time. But when we do you'll be the first person we call.'

Maisie studied my face, as if deciding whether I meant it. After a minute she seemed to make up her mind that I did, so she nodded and said, 'OK then. I can be all sorts of things, you know. Not just dogs. Maybe you could have a rabbit next time. I would be a very fantastic rabbit.' Not waiting for an answer, she started singing a song about a rabbit to herself and went back to flicking through her book. Hannah gave me a grateful smile.

'I won't stay long,' I said to her. 'I just had to tell you the exciting news. I asked Mum about the movie night and she said we can make it a sleepover!'

'Oh wow!' Hannah squealed. 'I've never been on a sleepover. Well, apart from at Granny's house I mean, but that doesn't count!'

'Will your mum let you come?' I asked, suddenly anxious.

'Oh, I'm sure she will, especially when it's only next door,' Hannah said. 'Oh my God, this is so exciting!'

'I know! I can't wait! OK, I'd better let you guys get back to your book. Let me know what your mum says, OK?'

I headed back home, my head buzzing with plans for Friday. We could all watch the movie tucked up in sleeping bags on the sitting room floor. We'd have popcorn and hot chocolate with marshmallows. We could paint each other's nails and put on temporary tattoos. It was going to be so much fun!

Chapter Eighteen

I couldn't wait for Friday to come – it was so exciting to think of our first Star Club sleepover! I had everything planned. We'd have our rehearsal first, then we'd decorate our own pizzas for dinner. After that we could paint our nails and go through the dressing-up box, trying things on to see what we had that could work for our show (and maybe Mum's wardrobe too, if she'd let us.) When it got late, we'd snuggle down in our sleeping bags in the sitting room and watch *Cinderella*.

Mum was almost as excited as me. She came home from work one day with a huge shopping bag, and she made me close my eyes and hold out my hands while she took out what she'd bought. I felt soft material being draped over my arms.

'OK, you can open your eyes!' Mum said.

I looked down to see that I was holding a pair of silky pyjamas, covered in pink and purple stars. 'Oh Mum, they're beautiful!'

'I got a pair for each of you,' Mum said, holding the bag open to show me. 'They can be your special Star Club sleepover pyjamas.'

'I love them,' I told her, giving her a hug.

Mum's eyes filled with tears. Sometimes she gets so emotional over the smallest things. 'I'm so glad, darling. I just want you to have a wonderful time with your friends!'

When Friday finally came I rushed home from school, not waiting to walk with Hannah and Ruby for once. I only had a few hours to get everything ready!

Mum had done a lovely job in decorating our house over the summer, even though it's rented. We had lovely fluffy cushions in the sitting room, soft curtains in a deep wine colour that gave the room a cosy feel, and she always kept the cut crystal glasses filled with fresh lilies. It was a beautiful grown-up room, but I wanted to give it a personal touch for the sleepover.

Quickly I set to work. First I hung bunting across the curtain rail – gorgeous patchwork patterns that Sadie had used one time for a garden party. I hung strings of pink fairy lights across the fireplace and twined another set around the bookshelves. I blew up balloons and strung them together in bunches to give the room a party feel. Finally I took all the candles I could find and arranged them on the mantelpiece, bookshelves and side tables. I'd have to promise Mum that I'd keep an eye on them, but I was sure she wouldn't mind when she saw how lovely and cosy I'd made the place look.

Mum exclaimed in delight when she came home from work and saw what I'd done. 'Oh Meg darling, you've done a fabulous job! Such lovely little touches. If you change your mind about being an actress you could have a wonderful career as a set designer!'

'I won't change my mind,' I told her, laughing, 'but this is quite fun too!'

'Oh, but candles?' Mum said, frowning slightly as she saw my arrangements.

'We'll be super careful,' I said quickly. 'I'll only light them when we're watching the film. I'll blow them out before we start any pillow fights or anything!'

'Oh, all right then. I trust you.' Mum kissed the top of my head.

Just then the doorbell rang. Mum squealed as if she was a schoolgirl being caught out of place by the principal.

'They're here! I'd better get started on those pizzas!'

She dashed off to the kitchen, leaving me to open the door.

Laura, Ruby and Hannah were all standing on the door-step carrying their overnight bags, looking as excited as I felt. We hugged each other as if we hadn't seen each other in three months instead of three hours.

'Come on in!' I told them. 'I'm so glad you're here! We're going to have pizza for dinner and then we can watch the film later.'

The girls crowded into the hall, all talking at the same time.

'Pizza, my favourite …'

'I can't wait to see the film …'

'This is so exciting, my first ever sleepover!'

'Look, I brought some nail stickers, we can do our nails later …'

I showed them where to leave their bags in the sitting room, then we went out to the garden for what might be our last outdoor rehearsal of the season.

It wasn't exactly our most productive rehearsal ever – we were a bit too hyper to concentrate – but not even Hannah seemed to care. When Mum called us in to choose toppings for our pizza we decided we'd had enough rehearsing for one day. I made my pizza into a face, giving it pepperoni eyes, a cherry tomato nose, a green pepper smile, sweetcorn freckles and mozzarella hair. Laura saw my pizza and started doing the same thing, only her eyes were made of mushrooms as she's a vegetarian. Ruby covered her pizza with as many different toppings as she could fit, and Hannah picked the only two toppings she likes – sweetcorn and peppers – and spread them evenly over her pizza.

While we were waiting for the pizzas to cook, I poured everyone some juice and we set the table. Mum hovered in the background, keeping an eye on the pizzas, but not interfering. She'd promised that once dinner was over she was going to go upstairs and stay out of our way. She planned to have a long hot bubble bath and then go to bed with her book. 'I wouldn't dream of cramping your style, darling,' she'd told me.

The pizzas were delicious. Ruby swore she couldn't eat another mouthful, but when I said we could make our own ice cream sundaes for dessert she suddenly found she had a bit of room left after all. We made them with three different types of ice cream and topped them with sprinkles and chocolate sauce. Afterwards we painted each other's nails and stuck on the sparkly nail stickers that Ruby had brought.

'How about we watch the film now?' I said at last, when everyone's nails were as fabulous as they could possibly be.

'Let's get into our pyjamas first,' Laura said.

'Oh, I have a surprise for you!' I told them. 'Look under your pillows.'

I had put pillows out for everyone and left them on top of their sleeping bags. The girls did what I said and there were more squeals of excitement when they found their starry pyjamas. Mum popped in to see what all the noise was about, and was delighted to see how well her presents had gone down.

'Oh, thank you, Cordelia, these are amazing!' Ruby said. 'Real Star Club pyjamas!'

'You're welcome, darlings,' Mum said, beaming around at everyone. 'Well, I'm off to have a nice long soak in the bath. Be good and try not to burn the house down, won't you?'

Once we had all changed into our pyjamas, and Laura had taken a selfie of the four of us on her phone, we got into our sleeping bags and I put the DVD on. I love *Cinderella* so much – it is just the most gorgeous film, with brilliant acting and a real magical feel, and it's pretty funny too.

It took us ages to watch the film because we kept wanting to pause or rewind so we could study an actor's expression or write down a line that might work in our show. Mum was right – you could learn so much from watching other actors. Hannah and I especially enjoyed watching the two ugly stepsisters, who were mean and cruel and funny all at once.

Ruby started yawning almost the second the film was over.

'Ruby, you can't be sleepy yet!' Laura told her. 'The night's only getting started.'

'I'm not sleepy,' Ruby said, stifling another yawn. 'I was just – stretching my jaw.'

'What should we do now?' I asked.

'Let's play "Would You Rather?"' Laura said at once.

'Ooooh, yes!' Ruby and Hannah said.

'How do you play that?' I asked, once again conscious of the fact that everyone seemed to know some ordinary childhood thing that I didn't.

They all practically fell over each other in their rush to explain it to me. Hannah talked the loudest so I ended up listening to her. 'You have to make up two awful scenarios, and everyone else has to choose which one they'd prefer – and you HAVE to choose one! So for example, would you rather be eaten by a lion or drown in a pool of snot?'

'Ewwww!' I cried.

'It's a gross game,' Laura said. 'You just have to roll with it.'

'It doesn't HAVE to be gross!' Ruby insisted. 'Like some of them can be more like a mind-boggling dilemma. Like, would you rather go to Disneyland and only get to go on the Dumbo ride and have to stay on it for two whole weeks, or never go to Disneyland ever in your whole entire life?'

'Oh no,' I said. 'I can't believe you're making me choose.'

'Would you rather ...' Hannah said, 'go into school in just your underwear, or have to kiss everyone in your class on the lips – including Miss Brennan?'

'OK, I've got one,' I said. 'Would you rather your

teacher turned into a hamster, or your hamster turned into a teacher?'

'That's easy,' Ruby said. 'I haven't got a hamster, so I'd much rather Miss Brennan turned into one. Couldn't you just picture her, running around in her little hamster wheel and nibbling on treats?'

We all began laughing at this crazy image. Then Laura said, 'OK, I've got another one. Would you rather eat a poisonous spider or your best friend's eyeball?'

'Laura! That's so disgusting!' Ruby said, throwing a stuffed elephant at her.

Laura immediately threw a pink rabbit at Ruby, but it missed and hit me instead. Within seconds we were all flinging cuddly toys and cushions at each other, until we were laughing so hard we had to stop.

Mum appeared at the door. Her hair was twisted into a bun on top of her head and she was wearing her favourite silver dressing gown. 'Is everyone still alive in here?'

'Yes thanks,' I said, giggling.

'Maybe it's time for a quieter game,' Mum said, eyeing the giant fluffy teddy bear which had somehow landed on top of the lampshade. 'How about I bring you in some hot chocolate, and you can think about settling down for the night? It's getting late.'

'Hot chocolate would be lovely, thanks,' said Hannah. 'And we'll calm down now, won't we guys?'

Hannah has the sort of reassuring manner grown-ups love. Mum smiled at her. 'Right, four hot chocolates coming up.'

When she had gone, we quickly tidied the room, putting the cushions back on the couches and the teddies back on our sleeping bags. We straightened lampshades and throws, and I stood up on the couch to retrieve Hannah's toothpaste, which had been flung right up on the top shelf of the bookcase. Mum came back to find a much calmer room and four girls sitting waiting for their hot chocolates.

'OK, I've got an idea for a nice quiet game,' Ruby said once we were sipping on our hot chocolates and Mum had gone. 'We all have to tell each other a secret that we've never shared before.'

'OK,' Laura said, 'but only if you go first.'

'Fine,' said Ruby, who had obviously thought this through. 'My ballet teacher says if I keep practising really hard she is going to put me in for my next grade exam after Christmas. I wasn't supposed to be doing it until the summer.' Ruby looked shy but proud of herself, which wasn't surprising.

'That's amazing, Ruby!' I said. 'Aren't you already a year ahead of girls your age?'

'Yes,' Ruby said, glowing. 'I'd be in with the fourteen- and fifteen-year-olds if I passed. Now you, Laura.'

'OK … you know that boy Andrea likes – Greg?'

We nodded. We'd heard all about Greg, who was on the basketball team in Andrea's secondary school. Andrea doesn't even like sport, but she had gone to every one of the team's matches this term just to watch Greg.

'Wellll,' Laura went on, 'I thought it was just a crush, I didn't think Greg even knew who Andrea was. But then when I was cycling home from Hannah's the other day I saw them in the park together – and they were kissing!'

'Aaaaagh!'

'Have you told her you saw them?' I asked.

'Not yet. I figured I'd wait and see if the information might prove valuable for some reason,' Laura said with a grin. 'OK, your turn, Hannah.'

'You know all my secrets,' Hannah complained. 'I've known you since we were about two!'

'There must be something,' Ruby insisted.

Hannah thought for a minute. 'OK. You know when Mum hurt her ankle and I was looking after the kids? Well, one day I'd made fish fingers and waffles for dinner, but Bobby said he didn't like fish fingers any more. So I told him they weren't fish fingers, they were shark fingers, and he ate them all up and said they were yummy. Now he keeps asking Mum for shark fingers and she doesn't know what he's talking about!'

'Good one,' Ruby said. 'OK, Meg, your turn.'

My heart was pounding. This was the perfect opportunity to just get it over with and tell them. They had to know some time, right? I started to say something, but at the last minute I chickened out. I just couldn't do it. 'Well, you see, my secret is that my mum is an actress, my dad is a film director and my granny and grandad are both in theatre too. Oh wait, I forgot. That's not a secret, because the whole town knows.'

Everyone laughed, and Hannah gave my arm a sympathetic rub.

'Nice try, Meg,' Laura said. 'We need a secret you haven't told us before. Something you haven't told anyone.'

I racked my brains for something safe I could tell them. 'Uh …'

'Are you girls still talking?'

I'd never been so thankful to see Mum appearing at the door.

'Come on now, snuggle down and go to sleep. It's after 1am! Your parents will never allow you to stay over again if I send you home exhausted!'

'Sorry, Mum,' I said. 'We'll go to sleep now.'

'Sorry, Cordelia,' everyone murmured.

Mum waited until we were all lying down, then turned off the last lamp.

'Goodnight, girls. Sleep well.' She squeezed my hand as she went by and I squeezed back, grateful for her perfect timing.

Ruby waited until she heard Mum's bedroom door close upstairs, then whispered sleepily, 'You owe us a secret, Meg.'

Chapter Nineteen

Next morning we all slept late. I woke up first, and tiptoed out of the sitting room so as not to wake the others. The kitchen clock said it was nearly ten o'clock!

'Morning, sleepyhead,' Mum said. She was already dressed and sitting at the kitchen table, drinking a cup of coffee and flicking through a magazine. 'Where are the girls?'

'Still asleep,' I told her. 'Can I make French toast for breakfast, Mum?' I loved making French toast – it was pretty easy, not to mention delicious.

'I thought you'd want to – I even got white bread,' Mum said, gesturing towards the bread bin. Since she'd started her healthy eating thing it had been wholemeal bread all the way. 'And there are plenty of eggs in the fridge.'

'Thanks, Mum.'

I cracked eggs into a bowl, stirred in milk and started dipping slices of bread into it. I melted some butter in a frying pan and when it was sizzling I dropped in a few slices of bread.

'Hey, you should have called us.' Hannah was at the kitchen door, her long brown hair all tousled, still looking pretty sleepy.

'I was going to,' I told her. 'I just thought I'd start break-fast first. I'm making French toast.'

'Yum! I'll call the other two.'

The words 'French toast' seemed to work like magic to get Ruby and Laura out of bed. A few minutes later we were all sitting around the kitchen table eating our tasty breakfasts, topped with maple syrup and some of Gran-dad's blackberries.

'When you've finished your breakfast,' Mum said, 'if you'd all like to get dressed quickly, I thought I would take you into town to do some shopping for costumes.'

'Oh, that would be brilliant!' Laura said. 'Miss Brennan wants us to do a dress rehearsal for the class on Monday, and I'm not sure we have what we need at home.'

'Don't you have ballet?' Hannah asked Ruby.

But Ruby shook her head. 'No, it's my private class on Saturday mornings, and Miss O'Neill moved it to Sunday this week.'

'Yay – so we can all go!' I said. 'Thanks, Mum!'

Half an hour later Mum parked the car outside the main shopping centre in Carrickbeg. 'So do you know where you want to go, ladies?'

'Let's try Claire's Accessories first,' Hannah said. 'And then Penney's.'

'And we could try that secondhand shop Sadie loves,' I suggested. 'They usually have some cool stuff.'

'And we'll have to hit the chemist for some make-up,' Ruby added.

'Sounds like this could take a while,' Mum said. 'Good thing I have plenty to keep me busy! There's a sale on in Shoe City. They had the most divine pair of red kitten heels the last day. I do hope they're reduced because I simply must have them! Now, you know where we're meeting for lunch, don't you darlings?'

'Yes Mum, you've only reminded me about four times,' I told her. 'We'll be there!'

'Well, make sure you are. Have fun, darlings!'

Mum strode off in the direction of Shoe City, and my friends and I turned to each other, feeling excited.

'Claire's then?' Laura said.

'Yes!'

Claire's was pretty quiet, which was just as well, because we were definitely not. Ruby started squealing with excitement over some hot pink tutus, and Laura started draping feather boas over her, while Hannah tried on a leopard-print cowboy hat with some oversized sunglasses that made her look a bit like she was in disguise. I found some stripy leggings in black and luminous green, which was just what I had in mind for Hepzibah, and a pair of black pointy glasses which would look great for Faye.

'Look, look, you have to try this on,' Hannah said, rushing up to me with a flowery hat. 'It would clash horribly!'

'And this!' Laura hung a purple feather boa around me.

Ruby came up too to add a gaudy scarf. I looked at myself in the mirror and started laughing – I looked ridiculous!

'OK, Hannah's turn, I don't want to be the only crazy one!' I said, and Laura and Ruby turned their attention to Hannah, who soon looked as funny as me.

'Don't look now, but I think the shop assistant might have had about enough of us,' Hannah said all of a sudden. 'Hey – I said don't look!'

Obviously you should never tell people not to look now, because that's exactly what they're going to do. An older lady behind the till was frowning over at us, and she turned and said something to her younger assistant, who moved over in our direction.

'Maybe we'd better just decide what we're buying,' Ruby said nervously. She hates getting in any kind of trouble.

'We're not doing anything wrong,' Laura said defiantly. 'We're customers, we're entitled to try things on before we make our minds up.' Nevertheless, she started putting back some of the feather boas.

'Can I help you girls with anything?' It was the younger assistant, a fake smile plastered to her face.

'Yes please,' Laura said, speaking in her Auntie Faye voice, and peering at the assistant over the top of the pointy glasses. 'I'm looking for some accessories for my two nieces.' She pointed to me and Ruby.

The assistant's eyebrows went up at the suggestion that twelve-year-old Laura was our aunt, but Laura carried on as if it was all perfectly normal. 'Now, as you can see they like to wear as many different colours and patterns as they can possibly find – it's how they express themselves, isn't it, darlings? Do you have this scarf in another pattern? Something with polka dots perhaps?'

'Uh – I think we have it in rainbow stripes, if you would like to take a look?' the shop assistant said.

'Delightful. Thank you.'

Laura managed to keep a straight face while the poor shop assistant brought her one thing after another. She made Hannah and me hold them up against us and turned her head on one side with a critical expression.

'Yes, I believe red is your colour, Hepzibah,' she told me. 'It brings out the red in your eyes.'

By now Hannah and I were really struggling not to laugh. Ruby had given up the battle and was hiding behind the earrings display, her hand tightly clamped over her mouth.

'Thank you, my dear,' Laura said to the shop assistant. 'I believe we have everything we need now. Let me just consult my nieces as to their favourite options and we will be over in just a little moment.'

'Of course.' The shop assistant looked extremely relieved to escape, scuttling back over to the till where her boss was looking crosser than ever.

'Laura, you're terrible!' Hannah told her, giggling.

'I thought she was going to kick us out of the shop,' I said.

'Is she gone?' Ruby poked her head around the earrings. 'Oh my God, Laura, I thought I was going to die laughing!'

'I'm sure I don't know what you mean,' Laura said, still in her Auntie Faye voice. 'Can't an aunt spoil her favourite ugly nieces?'

'OK, what are we going to buy?' Hannah asked. 'We haven't got enough money for everything.'

'Definitely these leggings anyway,' I said. 'And why don't you get the pink stripy ones? I think it would be cool if we had stuff that sort of matched.'

'And we have to have these crazy tutus,' Hannah said.

'And I NEED these pointy glasses,' Laura said in her normal voice. She still hadn't taken them off, even though the price tag dangling down the middle of the frame must have been tickling her nose.

'Absolutely,' I agreed.

We finally settled on the tutus, the leggings, two clashing wigs and the glasses. We figured we could find feather boas in Sadie's attic and someone was bound to have strings of beads in their jewellery box.

'We haven't got anything for you, Ruby,' I said.

'I haven't really seen anything,' Ruby said. 'Cindy's outfit should be more ordinary really, shouldn't it? We can look in Penney's.'

'Cool. Let's take this all to the till so before we get thrown out.'

We pooled all our money and Laura paid for everything, still being Auntie Faye, and telling the shop assistant she was 'too marvellous for words' and a 'perfect darling' for being so helpful.

She put on her Auntie Faye walk, wiggling her hips as she strolled towards the door, the rest of us scurrying after her. As soon as we were safely outside we burst into giggles, all except Laura, who widened her eyes at us and said, 'What? Hannah, you're always telling us to take every opportunity to get into character.'

We linked arms and wandered down in the direction of Penney's. But just as we reached the open space in the middle of the shopping centre, I saw it. Huge red letters declared 'COMING SOON' on an enormous film poster with a scene featuring two dark heads and two blonde ones. In smaller but still very prominent letters was the line 'Starring Michael Cooper, Daniel Stephens, Cordelia Sheridan and Daisy Sheridan.' I barely glanced at the men's faces because the taller blonde was, unmistakeably, Mum.

And the smaller one was me.

Chapter Twenty

I froze. Ruby on one side of me and Laura on the other were both still walking so my sudden stop jerked their arms.

'Oh, s-sorry,' I stammered, slipping my hands back into their arms. My heart was racing and I hoped that somehow, somehow, they hadn't seen the poster. But on the other side of Laura Hannah had stopped too and was staring straight ahead, open-mouthed.

'Meg,' she said. 'Meg, it's you!'

Ruby and Laura followed Hannah's gaze and stopped dead too. All three of them stared at the poster, unable to believe their eyes. As the Saturday crowds swirled around us, Hannah began moving towards the poster to get a closer look, and the other two followed. I stayed where I was, completely rooted to the spot.

Finally the girls stopped staring at the poster and crowded around me instead.

'YOU'RE Daisy Sheridan?' Ruby said, sounding completely incredulous.

'Why didn't you tell us?' Laura asked.

'You're actually in a FILM,' Ruby said.

I couldn't say anything. It was like my voice was as frozen as my legs.

Hannah took charge. 'Come on, let's go in here for hot chocolate. I think we all need a sit-down!'

She took my arm and steered me into a café, choosing a table in a quiet corner well away from the window. Ruby and Laura were still staring at me as if my hair had suddenly turned green or I had horns coming out of my head or something. Hannah managed to get the attention of the waitress and ordered four hot chocolates. Once the waitress had gone she turned to me.

'So what's going on, Meg? It is you in the poster, isn't it?'

I nodded. They waited for me to go on. The chatter of other customers and the clinking of cutlery and the hiss of the coffee machine all seemed to fade into the background as I finally found my voice. 'Yes, it's me. It's my dad's new film. Mum and I are both in it.'

'You're actually a film star,' Ruby said, shaking her head in disbelief.

I gave a shaky laugh. 'I wouldn't call me a star. It's not a very big part. I think they've only put me on the poster because of the whole mother-daughter thing.'

'So what's the part?' Hannah asked.

'It's a political thing,' I told them. 'For grown-ups, you know – pretty dull, to be honest. Mum plays a politician who's running for office and these two men are conspiring against her. I play her daughter – I'm only in a couple of scenes. Honestly, it's a really tiny part. I don't know why they've put me on the poster. It's probably just because of the family name.'

Hannah pounced on this. 'Yes, the name! Why are you called Daisy Sheridan? Your name is Meg Howard – or is that some sort of disguise this whole time?'

'No, of course not,' I said. 'My real name is Margaret – I did tell you that when I met you first. And Meg and Daisy are both nicknames for Margaret. It's my aunt's name, my dad's sister. My dad didn't want it at first because he thought it was kind of an old lady name. But Mum liked it because of all the different short forms. She said it would give me the chance to be lots of different people if I wanted to.' I smiled wanly – I bet even Mum couldn't have foreseen the way that would turn out.

'But your surname?' Ruby asked.

'Howard is my dad's name, so that's what I normally use,' I said. 'But Mum's surname is Sheridan, and because she's from an acting family the film producers wanted me to use their name too. Dad wasn't too happy at first, but he saw that it made sense. Mum's family are a lot more famous than he is – at least, they have been up until now. And it meant I could keep my identity as an actress separate from my private life.'

The other girls were quiet for a moment, taking it all in. All around us the café was filled with the happy sounds of Saturday shoppers coming in to have a little break from their shopping and show each other what they'd been buying. It was hard to believe that in such an ordinary setting we were having such an extraordinary conversation.

Laura finally spoke for the first time. 'Why didn't you tell us, Meg? We'd have been so excited for you. We ARE so excited for you!'

I blushed. 'I'm sorry. I wanted to, but you know how crazy everything was in school when it came out about Mum and Dad. I thought I'd just have a few more months before it all had to come out about the new film.'

'You mean you weren't expecting anything like this?' Ruby said, waving her arm in the general direction of the poster, even though – thankfully – we couldn't see it from where we were sitting.

'No, I had no idea,' I said. 'The film wasn't supposed to be coming out until the spring.'

'Oh my God – so you didn't know these posters were suddenly going to appear?' Hannah said.

'No.' I suddenly thought of Mum, off shopping for

shoes and blissfully unaware that a bombshell was about to strike. 'Oh my God, Mum is going to go absolutely crazy. She's going to KILL Dad!'

'You mean your dad is behind all this?'

Hannah's voice sounded shocked. I didn't blame her. I was pretty shocked myself. Even by Dad's standards, this was pretty low.

The waitress arrived with our hot chocolates. I sipped the hot, creamy liquid, grateful for the warmth that spread through me, a bit of comfort. I realised I was shaking – the cup rattled against the saucer as I tried to set it back down.

'Mum and Dad have been fighting about this for weeks now,' I told the girls. 'Dad kept wanting me to go back out to LA to do some promotional work for the film – interviews with the press, getting my photo taken, all that sort of thing. Mum didn't want me to – I'd only just started school here, and she wanted me to have a chance to settle in properly. He kept pestering her too about choosing photos for press releases and all sorts of things. We couldn't understand what the rush was – Mum just kept putting him off. Now of course I can see why he was being so insistent.'

'So your dad knew all along that the film was coming out now?' Ruby asked, eyes wide with shock.

'He must have done,' I said miserably. 'And he must have known Mum wouldn't be happy. So much for me settling into school as a normal kid. Not much chance of that if my photo is going to be all over town!'

'Maybe people won't realise it's you,' Ruby said doubtfully. 'I mean, the name and everything ...' Her voice trailed off. I don't think she was even convincing herself.

'You recognised me from halfway across the shopping centre,' I pointed out.

The girls were quiet for a minute. Then Laura said, 'You know what we need here? Damage limitation.'

'What do you mean?' I asked, feeling a spark of hope at Laura's positive tone.

'If you tell everyone yourself, you can make it less of a shock,' Laura said. 'When Miss Brennan asks us about our news on Monday morning, tell the class about the film then.'

'Yes! That makes sense,' Hannah said. 'That way people would get to hear it like you've told us – you know, that it's a small part in a small film – not a huge blockbuster or something. You could tell the story the way you want to instead of leaving it all to gossip and rumours.'

'That's if everyone hasn't already seen the posters,' Ruby muttered.

'Maybe they won't have. Maybe there's only the one poster,' I said, feeling hopeful. I really wanted to believe Laura's plan would work – that it could all be played down if I handled it right. Maybe Dad wasn't the only one in our family who could spin a story the way they wanted to.

'I'm surprised Tracey didn't know already, actually,' Ruby said. 'You know, with her aunt being a journalist and everything.'

Hannah snorted. 'Mum says you can't call what she does journalism. She's just a gossip columnist, always spying on celebrities.'

A cold chill swept over me. 'Tracey's aunt?' I said. 'Are you sure?'

'Yes, she's always telling us stories she's heard about this celebrity or that one,' Hannah said. 'Half of them are made up.'

'I did wonder if she was the one who told everyone about your mum and dad,' Laura said.

'No, she can't have been,' I said. 'She was actually upset that I hadn't told her first. Although ...' I stopped, remembering how Tracey had later insisted to Jamie that she had known.

Ruby looked confused. 'But I thought Isabel said she'd been talking to Tracey about it that morning before school. In fact, I'm sure Isabel said she'd heard it from Tracey in the first place.'

'But that doesn't make any sense,' I said, feeling as confused as Ruby looked. 'Why would she tell people and then pretend to me that she hadn't known?'

Hannah, Ruby and Laura were all looking at each other

as if each of them was hoping someone else would answer.

'What's going on, guys?' I asked. 'Do you all know something I don't?'

Hannah spoke hesitantly. 'We didn't know whether we should say anything. You seemed to be getting on well with Tracey, and we didn't want to sort of turn you against her or whatever. But she's been pretty mean to us a few times in the past. She's nice to people's faces, but then says horrible things about them behind their backs. Well, except for me. She's horrible to my face too – but usually only when there aren't other people from school around.'

'I guess she has more opportunities to be mean to you because you live so near each other,' Ruby said. She turned to me. 'She's always mocking things like Hannah being from a big family and everything. As if there's anything wrong with that!'

'She's too sneaky to be nasty in front of big groups of people,' Laura said shrewdly. 'It doesn't go with the image she's trying to give off. Or what she'll do is, she'll say something that sounds like a compliment but she's actually being mean. Like she said to me one time, "That's a lovely dress you're wearing. My granny has one just like it." She wants people to think she's nice, but she's really just looking out for number one. And she's a bit obsessed with celebrities, actually.'

'Oh my God. I had no idea,' I said, my mind racing. This

could explain so much. And if Tracey really had known about my parents before everyone else, maybe that was why she had been so keen to be friends with me? Maybe – and this was a truly freaky thought – she had actually known that I was Daisy Sheridan all along?

Ruby voiced what I was thinking. 'Do you think she knew you were Daisy Sheridan? Maybe she heard about you from her aunt, and she wants to be friends with you because you're famous.'

'Maybe she's spying on you for her aunt!' Laura said, her eyes widening. 'Looking for bits of gossip she can pass on, hoping she might be invited to your house or even to some celebrity party.'

I remembered what I'd overheard Tracey saying, that I was going to invite her to a film premiere. Maybe that wasn't just something she'd made up to impress Jamie – maybe it was something she was really trying to engineer.

'Oh Laura, not spy stories again!' Hannah said, groaning. 'You've got a wild imagination. No one would go to those lengths – not even Tracey.'

But I wasn't so sure. 'They would, you know,' I said slowly. 'I've heard all sorts of stories like that. An actress Mum knows started going out with a guy who seemed really nice, but she found out later that he was telling the paparazzi where they'd be going on dates so they could come along and take photos. He wasn't really interested in her as a person at all. This is what I was afraid of, in a way, and why Mum was so keen for me to keep my identity secret at school. Once people know you're famous, it's hard to know who your real friends are, and who's just hanging around with you because they want a bit of the glamour and excitement.'

I could tell from my friends' faces that they were convinced – even Hannah.

'Well, whatever happens, you can count on us, Meg,' she told me, and the other two chimed in in agreement. 'We're Star Club – and we stick together.'

Chapter Twenty-one

Our hot chocolates were long since finished. The waitress was hovering over our table, obviously keen to clear it with other shoppers waiting to sit down.

'What time is it?' I asked. 'We're supposed to meet Mum.'

Hannah checked her watch. 'Eek, we're late.'

'Don't say anything to Mum, will you?' I asked my friends. 'About the poster, I mean. Hopefully she hasn't seen it. I'd rather tell her at home, when we're on our own. She's going to be so shocked.'

'We won't,' Ruby promised.

'We'd better get going,' I said. 'We've been here ages! And we didn't even get a chance to shop for an outfit for you, Ruby.'

'That's OK,' Ruby said. 'I'll ask Mum to bring me tomorrow after ballet.'

Mum was waiting outside Cowtown Café, several bulging shopping bags at her feet. She was humming to herself as she looked around for us, and she seemed so relaxed I knew she couldn't have seen the poster.

'Sorry we're late, Mum,' I told her. 'We were chatting and lost track of time.'

'Oh, you girls and your chatting!' Mum said, rolling her eyes, but not looking at all cross. 'Never mind, let's get a seat, shall we? I'm ready for some lunch after my busy morning of shopping. Actually, I'm gasping for a cup of tea.'

'Did you get the shoes?' I asked, examining the bags.

'Yes – in red *and* in silver,' Mum confessed. 'I simply couldn't resist. They're too adorable for words!'

We showed Mum everything we'd bought too, and she made me and Hannah try on our ugly stepsister accessories while we waited for our lunch to arrive. Laura put on her Auntie Faye voice to order lunch which Mum thought was hilarious – she had no idea Laura was modelling it on her.

We had so much fun I managed to put the film poster right out of my mind. It was only when we were driving home that I started to worry about how I was going to tell Mum the news.

'Well, this has been fabulous, darlings, but I'd better get you home,' Mum told my friends. 'Your parents will be thinking I've kidnapped you!'

Ruby stifled a giggle, and I knew she was thinking of

the time Laura was convinced Mum had kidnapped me.

Mum took no notice. 'I'll drop Hannah and Ruby home first, then you, Laura, because Meg and I are going to see her grandparents.'

'Oh, great,' I said. Maybe it would be easier to break the news to Mum with Sadie and Grandad around for support.

'I think Grandad wants you to read Ophelia's lines for him again, darling,' Mum told me. 'No rest for the wicked!'

She pulled up outside Ruby's house, and Ruby and Hannah got out.

'Thanks so much, Cordelia,' Ruby said. 'I had a fabulous time.'

'Me too,' Hannah said. Then she whispered to me, 'Good luck!' before waving us off.

We dropped Laura home and then Mum parked outside Sadie's house. We were just getting out of the car when Sadie came rushing out of the house, waving a newspaper at us. 'Cordelia! Why didn't you tell us?'

Chapter Twenty-two

'Tell you what?' Mum pushed her sunglasses up on her head, looking puzzled.

'About the film, of course!'

'She doesn't know, Sadie,' I said quickly.

'I don't know what?' Mum demanded. She looked from me to Sadie and then back to me again, her expression changing from bewildered to cross. 'Will someone please tell me what's going on?'

'Let's go inside,' I said. The last thing I wanted was for Laura to be spying on us from across the road. It wouldn't be the first time she'd used her location across from Sadie's to mount a secret spying mission.

Mum took no notice, taking the paper from Sadie and scanning it quickly. Looking over her shoulder, I saw the same image from the film poster we'd seen in town, taking up a whole page in the newspaper.

'Oh my God,' Mum said, the colour draining from her

face. 'Oh my GOD! I'm going to bloody kill him!'

She scrunched up the newspaper in her hand and stalked into the house, leaving Sadie and me to look at each other in shock.

'She really didn't know?' Sadie asked.

'No,' I said softly.

'But you did?'

I shook my head. 'I saw a poster in town this morning, that's the first I heard of it. Dad must have given the go-ahead without asking Mum.'

Sadie's eyebrows shot up. 'Good heavens. No wonder Cordelia's annoyed. Come on, let's go in.'

Inside, Mum had picked up Sadie's landline and was pushing her finger into the keypad as if she wanted to stab it.

'Cordelia, why don't you have a nice cup of tea first?' Sadie said in a soothing tone. 'I'll put the kettle on.'

'No thanks, Sadie,' Mum said through clenched teeth. 'Tea isn't going to solve this one.' She tapped her foot impatiently, waiting for Dad to answer the phone.

'Yes, I bloody know what time it is!' she said into the phone.

Sadie's hall clock read half past two. That meant it was just half past six in Los Angeles. Dad would have been fast asleep and certainly not expecting to be woken by an angry phone call.

'What do you think you're playing at, Doug?' Mum was practically screaming now. 'How dare you put our daughter's photo on that poster without my permission? You know I'm supposed to have approval on anything like that. I specifically put it in her contract that publicity work had to go through me! And when were you planning on telling me that the film's release date had been brought forward? Did you just think it was a good idea to let me find out from the sodding newspaper?'

Sadie put her arm around my shoulder and guided me into the kitchen. 'Come on, darling,' she whispered. 'I'm sure you could do with a cup of tea even if Mum doesn't want one.'

I went into the kitchen with Sadie, torn between wanting to know what was going on and not wanting to hear Mum and Dad screaming at each other.

Grandad was pacing up and down the garden, his script in his hand. He saw me through the kitchen window and came in, smiling. 'Hello, poppet. Where's your mum?'

'On the phone to Dad,' I said.

Sadie quickly told Grandad what was going on, moving back and forth across the kitchen making a pot of tea as she did so. Grandad's frown grew deeper as Sadie explained.

I sank down in a chair, suddenly feeling exhausted. Grandad came over and sat beside me, taking my hand in his. 'There now pet, don't you worry. Mum and Dad will sort it out.'

'They can't though, can they?' I said. 'It's too late. Dad's totally gone behind Mum's back, and it's not like we can take down the posters or burn all the newspapers, is it? Everyone in school is going to see this, and I'm going to have no chance of just being a normal kid.'

Grandad sighed and looked to Sadie for help. Sadie came over and sat down on the other side of me, rubbing my back. 'Well, maybe not, but you were never going to be just a normal kid, now were you, Meg?' she asked me. 'I said all along that it was unrealistic of Cordelia to think you could be, with your talent. Why, from the moment you could talk you could copy all the voices on your TV programmes – don't you remember, John?'

'I certainly do,' Grandad said. 'You had Peppa Pig down to perfection – I used to think there was a little English piggy in my sitting room, telling her brother not to be silly.'

In spite of myself I laughed at the memory. I used to love Peppa Pig and the way she jumped up and down in muddy puddles, and I did remember trying to copy her voice from when I was very small.

'I used to wish I could be Peppa Pig,' I said. 'And then Cinderella, and Sophie from *The BFG*, and Roberta from *The Railway Children*.'

'And that's the beauty of being an actress, darling,' Sadie

said. 'You get a chance to be all these different people, live all these different lives instead of just the one.'

'I know,' I said. 'I love that. It's just the other stuff I could happily live without.'

'It kind of goes with the territory, though,' Sadie said, patting my hand. 'Being an actress means living in the spotlight – at least, if you want to really succeed at it.'

'But I don't know if I really do want it, if that's what it means.' I turned to Grandad. 'Grandad, it's like you always say, it's the thrill of the live audience that makes it so special for me. I don't want to be in the newspaper or see my poster up in town when I'm shopping with my friends. None of that stuff matters to me. I don't mind being Daisy when I'm on the stage – but I just want to be Meg the rest of the time.'

'We know, poppet,' Grandad said.

None of us said anything for a minute. Sadie gave everyone a hot drop of tea, and offered me a biscuit, but I shook my head – I didn't feel like eating.

'I still can't believe Dad would do this without telling us,' I said at last. 'And without telling Mum!'

'I'm sure your dad had his reasons, dear,' Sadie said. 'Cordelia isn't always the easiest person to deal with, I'll be the first to admit that.'

'You don't have to stick up for him,' I told her. 'I'm totally on Mum's side here.'

'I'm glad to hear it.' Mum had come into the kitchen just in time to hear what I'd said.

Sadie poured her a cup of tea and Mum took a big sip before asking, 'Did you know about this, Meg?'

'Not until today,' I said. 'I saw a poster in town. I was going to tell you when we got here.'

Mum leaned over and hugged me. 'You poor darling. You must have been so worried. Where did you see the poster? What did your friends say?'

I told Mum everything, including Laura's 'damage limitation' plan. Mum perked up at once when she heard this.

'That sounds like an excellent idea. Clever Laura,' she said.

'Mum … what about Dad?' I asked.

'What about him?' Mum asked, tapping on the table with her long polished fingernail.

'Just … are you guys OK?'

Mum gave a little laugh. 'Depends what you mean by OK.'

'Now don't you worry, darling,' Sadie said. 'Mum and Dad will sort things out. Won't you, Cordelia?' she added in a warning tone.

'Yes, yes, of course,' Mum said. 'Don't worry, darling. This will all blow over.'

I hoped she was right.

Chapter Twenty-three

The rest of Saturday was pretty quiet. Feeling pretty shellshocked after all the craziness, I didn't want to go out again, just pottered around the house.

On Sunday morning we woke up to lashing rain. Mum and I stayed in our pyjamas and curled up on the couch to watch TV, glad we didn't need to go outside. Mum put on *Strictly Come Dancing*, which we'd recorded the night before because I was too tired to stay up after the sleepover. It's our favourite programme to watch together – we each have our favourite stars and we give everyone marks on their performance and try to guess what the judges will say.

'That's got to be the best dance so far,' Mum said, as a guy from a boy band hugged his partner after they finished their jive.

'Oh, no!' I said. 'It wasn't as good as the rhumba by that TV chef. And the weather lady's cha-cha-cha was even better!'

'No way!' said Mum. 'Look at the hip action! Divine, darling. Ah, if I was twenty years younger ...'

'Mum!' I protested. 'Gross!'

Just then we heard a rustling noise outside and the sound of a key being put in the door.

I looked at Mum. 'Are you expecting Sadie?'

'No.' Mum threw aside the blanket she had wrapped around her, got up and went to the sitting room door. I followed her.

Dad was standing in the hall, rain dripping off his light jacket, his wet hair matted to his head. He held out his arms. 'My two favourite girls!'

I held back a little, fully expecting Mum to start shouting again. But instead she ran to him and threw herself into his arms, crying 'Doug darling!' and not seeming to care in the least that her pyjamas were getting all wet. Dad held her tight and kissed her hair and her face and murmured into her ear while she clung onto him.

At last the two of them seemed to remember that I was there too. 'Meg, come and give your old man a hug,' Dad said, holding out one arm to me while still holding tight to Mum with the other.

I hesitated a moment, but then moved in, letting Dad put his arm around me too.

'I'm so sorry, Meg,' Dad said into my hair. 'I'm sorry, Cordelia. I never meant for you to find out the way you did. I felt terrible when I got your phone call yesterday. After you hung up I booked the first flight home that I could get.'

'That's so romantic,' Mum breathed.

I rolled my eyes. Yesterday she had been ready to kill him – and now this. The two of them were like a pair of teenagers sometimes.

'How about we go out for a nice brunch, and I'll explain everything to you?' Dad suggested, letting go of us at last to take off his wet jacket. 'Isn't there a diner just up the road?'

'Good idea,' Mum said. 'Meg, why don't you run upstairs and get dressed, darling.'

'Fine.' I stomped off upstairs. Mum might be ready to forgive and forget – but I wasn't. Not yet, anyway.

* * *

Over pancakes in the Rainbow Diner, Dad explained (or tried to) why the film was coming out so soon. The producer had had a change of heart and decided it would do better in the autumn, so it had been a huge rush for everyone involved to get the film ready for release.

'I've known for a while now that it would be an autumn release instead of a spring one,' he admitted. 'But I thought we were talking November – just in time for the Christmas market, you know?'

'November would have been so much better,' Mum sighed. 'Meg would have had two whole months in her new school as just Meg. Now she's barely had two weeks, and she has to face the attention of being a film star!'

'I know,' Dad said, squeezing my hand. 'I'm sorry, Meg. But it was out of my hands.'

'And to find out like this!' Mum went on. I was glad to see she'd rediscovered a little bit of her irritation at least. 'Walking through a shopping centre with her friends and suddenly seeing herself on a great big poster! And Sadie telling me about it after she saw it in the newspaper! Really, Doug, what were you thinking?'

'I'm sorry,' Dad said again. 'I did try to tell you last week on the phone, but you might remember you hung up on me.' He tried his famous puppy-dog expression on Mum, but she was having none of it.

'Don't even think about trying to turn this on me!' she said. 'You could have tried a bit harder! Anyway, that was days ago! You had plenty of opportunities since then.'

'I know,' Dad said, spreading his hands out with an air of resignation. 'I guess I just stuck my head in the sand and hoped it would all go away.'

'Typical,' Mum said, but her voice was a bit softer now.

Dad took her hand in his. Mum's hand looked so small

in his big ones.

'We're here now, so let's try to make the best of it, will we?' he said, his voice pleading. 'It's all happening sooner than we would have liked — but we always knew it was going to happen. Our Meg was always destined to be a shining star in the acting world.'

They both turned and smiled at me, and even though I was trying to stay cross I couldn't help smiling too.

'And besides, this is a good thing!' Dad said, seeming to grow in confidence, now that it looked like we were pre-pared to forgive him. 'Now everyone will get the chance to see how wonderful you are, Meg! You'll have the critics eating out of your hand.'

'I can't wait to see it on the big screen!' Mum said. 'I wonder if my hair looks all right.'

'Well, that's my other bit of news,' Dad said. 'You won't have to wait to see it on the big screen. The premiere is scheduled for Thursday, and I have the precious golden tickets for us to attend!'

Thursday! That was the day before our Cinderella per-formance. I'd have to have everything organised for the next morning before we went, I thought to myself.

'Ooh, fabulous!' Mum said. 'We'll have to go shopping. I've got absolutely nothing to wear.'

'Why don't you take Meg shopping now ...' Dad said, 'and I'll go home and book our flights.'

'Flights?' I asked.

'Yes, didn't I mention?' Dad said. 'The premiere is in LA.'

Chapter Twenty-four

On Monday morning, I put my costume and all my accessories into my schoolbag. Mum gave me a lift to school. We had planned it so that I got there a little later than usual. I didn't want to have to tell my story dozens of times to different groups in the yard. I was planning to do like Laura had suggested and just tell everyone in one go at news time.

'Good luck, darling, I'll be thinking of you,' Mum said, blowing me a kiss. She didn't drive off right away, but sat in the car watching as I walked in the school gate. It felt good knowing she was there.

The bell rang and I ran to join my line, glad we'd managed to time it right. If other kids had seen the posters or the newspaper ads, I didn't have to know about it just yet.

When Miss Brennan asked if anyone wanted to share some news from the weekend, I put my hand up straight away. Miss Brennan looked surprised. Probably because I hadn't put my hand up for anything, I thought to myself, never mind sharing news.

'Yes, Meg?' she said.

Hannah had turned around in her seat and was smiling encouragingly at me. I took a deep breath. 'Before I moved to Carrickbeg I lived in Los Angeles for a while, and when I was there I had a part in a film,' I said. 'It's called *Power Struggle*. It's not a very big part, but it was fun to do. And now the film is about to come out, so it will be in the cinemas soon.'

There were gasps all around the classroom. I glanced over at Tracey, who just looked bored.

'How wonderful, Meg,' Miss Brennan said. 'What's the film about?'

'It's about three politicians all fighting for the top job,' I told her. 'My mum plays one of them, and I play her daughter.'

'It sounds fantastic,' Miss Brennan said. 'I can't wait to see it. So, does anyone else have any news?'

And just like that it was over and done with. I listened as Aaron told Miss Brennan how his team had won their soccer match on Saturday, and Aoife described how she'd been at her cousin's birthday party.

'Well, what a lot of good news we have to share today,' Miss Brennan said. 'Exciting times for lots of the class. And now we have our performance to look forward to on Friday! So please line up at the door now, we're going down to the hall to practise our songs. And then we'll have the dress rehearsal of *Cinderella*!'

Miss Brennan was amazing. I couldn't believe how she had handled the whole thing. And now I got to put it all out of my head for a while, and concentrate on our dress rehearsal!

The four of us watched the rest of the class singing their first song, then Miss Brennan excused us so we could go and change. Filled with excitement, we gathered up our costumes and made for the girls' toilets. Ruby showed us the outfit her mum had bought her for the disco scene – a very short silver dress.

'That's so cool!' I told her.

'And you'll get to wear it again, too,' Hannah said. 'I'm not sure we're going to get a whole lot of wear out of these leggings, Meg.'

She pulled the stripy leggings out of her bag, and we giggled again at how hideous they were. Soon we'd managed to make ourselves look almost unrecognisable. I had a scarlet wig, a purple feather boa, and the horrible green stripy leggings. Hannah wore a very similar outfit, but in different colours – her feather boa was orange, her leggings were pink and black stripes, and her wig was electric blue. Both of us were dripping in beads and sequins, as over the top as we could make ourselves look. Ruby was wearing a dowdy brown dress that had come from Sadie's attic. It was frayed at the bottom and had patches sewn on. The dress was baggy enough that she could wear the silver dress underneath, so she could change quickly for the disco scene. Laura looked much older in her pointy glasses, skinny jeans and a glittery top, stumbling slightly in her high heels.

Miss Brennan knocked on the door. 'Are you girls nearly ready? Your audience is waiting.'

Ruby squealed in alarm. 'I've forgotten the disco ball, Miss! It's still in the classroom.'

'Don't worry,' Miss Brennan said soothingly. 'I'll go and get it while you set everything else up. I'm really looking forward to seeing this performance.'

'Don't forget your other costume,' Hannah said to Laura as we gathered up our props. Like Ruby, Laura would have to change for the disco scene, swapping her top and high heels for a boy's shirt and trainers, and tucking her long black hair underneath a short brown wig.

'Got it,' Laura said, patting her bag. 'Come on, let's go!'

In the corridor outside the hall, we could hear the class talking at full volume, taking advantage of the fact that Miss Brennan hadn't come back yet. We went through the stage door and into the wings, taking a sneaky peek at our classmates waiting in the hall. I felt the familiar surge of adrenalin before a performance, longing to throw myself into the part. At the same time, I was glad it was only our own class we were performing for now. It was a bit less daunting than performing for the whole school and all the visitors for the School Centenary would be. That's if I got to take part, I reminded myself. I squashed down that thought, determined to focus on my performance.

Miss Brennan appeared behind us with the disco ball. 'Now, have you got everything?'

'I think so,' Hannah told her. 'We're going to use that folding table for the soft drinks table, and we've got the sheet hung up behind it – they're behind the second set of curtains, so they won't show in the early scenes.' She showed Miss Brennan the sheet, which Hannah and her brothers had painted with silhouettes for the disco scene.

'It looks wonderful,' Miss Brennan told her. 'All right, get set up there and I'll go and settle down this noisy lot!'

She stepped out in front of the curtain and the class immediately fell silent. Miss Brennan was a kind, warm sort of person, I thought, but she also knew exactly how to make the class fall into line.

'Now children, remember this is a dress rehearsal, which means we behave exactly as if it's the real show. We run through the whole thing without stopping. Meg, Laura, Hannah and Ruby are all ready and waiting to give us a fantastic performance, and we're going to be a fantastic audience too, aren't we?'

The class responded with a big round of applause and there were even some cheers from some of the noisier people. I gulped. I hoped we could live up to their expectations.

The curtains swung back, and it was time to begin.

The first scene went wonderfully. Hannah and I got straight into our parts, jeering and mocking Cindy, talking in screechy voices and trying to outdo each other. I couldn't believe how different Hannah was from her usual friendly self – she had really thrown herself into the role. I wondered if I was doing as well as she was. Then I heard the audience laughing loudly at one of my lines, and immediately I felt better. After all the times we'd said those lines just between the four of us, it was so great to get the reaction of an audience to whom it was all new. Ruby was such a contrast to the ugly stepsisters, looking lonely and bedraggled in her torn dress. I was thrilled to see that the movements I'd helped her come up with really did help to convey the fact that she was totally subdued by their bullying.

Before I knew it, our first scene was over, and Hannah and I left the stage, calling insults to Cindy as we headed to the disco. Laura tottered onto the stage, her heels making a clacking sound. 'Cindy, darling, whatever is the matter?' she exclaimed. 'Now do dry those tears and tell your Auntie Faye all about it.'

In the wings, I smiled at Hannah. Laura really did sound exactly like my mum! We were glad to have a little breather and a chance to watch the other two acting. We could almost see Ruby, as Cindy, swell in confidence as her cool aunt told her, 'Cindy, you SHALL go to the disco!'

There was a short scene before the disco bit with just Hannah and me on the stage, giving the other two a chance to quickly change their costumes. My initial nerves were gone, and I relaxed into the role, enjoying the interaction with Hannah and how we brought out the best in each other's performance.

The disco scene was the best. Ruby drifted onto the stage, looking gorgeous in her new outfit, and as light as a feather as she floated through her dance.

'Who does she think she is?' Hannah exclaimed. 'She looks so plain. She's not even wearing any beads!'

'I know!' I responded, as the audience laughed. 'What a fashion disaster! She clearly doesn't know anything about how to put an outfit together!' I twirled my feather boa as I spoke and the audience laughed again.

'The boys are never going to notice her!' Hannah sneered.

That was Laura's cue to come on. Looking completely different, she strode onto the stage in her boy outfit and started chatting Ruby up. Hannah and I looked on in disgust and started making lots of jealous remarks.

Although the class had seen bits of our show before, they hadn't seen the ending. Our original twist to the story, where Cindy decides she's going to go off and live with Auntie Faye, went down really well, and Isabel and Aoife cheered. As Ruby finished her final line, everyone broke into applause. We looked at each other, thrilled with how well it had all gone, and grabbed each other's hands to take a bow together.

'That was wonderful, girls!' Miss Brennan said. 'Wasn't it, class? You're going to be the stars of School Centenary day.'

Just like that, the joy at our great performance disappeared, and the agonising knowledge that I had to make a choice rose up within me once again. I knew I couldn't keep it from my friends any longer. 'Can you guys meet me behind the hedge at break time?' I said as we started to tidy up. 'There's something else I have to tell you.'

Chapter Twenty-five

At break time I made sure Tracey wasn't watching before sneaking off to the junior yard. The other girls were already there, squeezed into the little hiding place.

'There must be a better place we can meet than this,' Laura said. 'Somewhere we can actually breathe would be nice.'

'We won't stay long,' I promised. 'I just needed to tell you something that I don't want everyone knowing.'

'I've never known a girl with so many secrets,' Laura muttered, but Hannah shushed her.

'What is it, Meg?' she asked.

I sighed. 'Dad wants me and Mum to go back to LA with him for the premiere of the film.'

'Oh wow, that's so exciting!' Ruby said. 'What are you going to wear?'

'You are going to go, aren't you?' Laura asked, seeing my hesitation.

'I want to, of course,' I said, 'even though I kind of hate the thought of all the press and everything. But the thing is, it's on Thursday.'

'*This* Thursday?' asked Hannah, looking distraught. 'In LA?'

'Yes,' I said, feeling terrible as my friends' faces all fell. 'I haven't decided anything yet,' I told them quickly. 'I really don't want to miss the show. We've put so much work in, and we were all looking forward to it so much. And especially after that dress rehearsal – it went so well, I feel like I can't wait to perform for real now!'

'But it's the premiere of your first film,' Hannah said. 'You can't miss that.'

'I have to miss one of them,' I said.

'What did your mum and dad say?' Ruby asked.

'They've said it's up to me,' I said. 'Dad can't understand why I'd even think about missing the premiere, but he shut up when Mum told him he had no right to start laying down the law after the stunt he'd pulled last week.' I grinned, thinking of Dad's hangdog expression when Mum told him to butt out and let me make up my own mind. 'Mum said it's totally up to me and she'll support me either way.'

'I hate when parents say that,' Hannah commented. 'It sounds like they're doing you a favour, but sometimes it would just be so much easier if they told you what you had to do.'

'That's all part of growing up, darling,' Laura said in her Auntie Faye voice, which made us all laugh.

'Anyway,' I said, 'I just wanted to let you know. I'm not asking you what I should do, or anything …'

'Oh good, because I don't know either!' said Hannah. 'It's like a really horrible game of "Would You Rather?"!'

'Except that both options are lovely,' Ruby pointed out.

They all looked at me, waiting for me to say something else. I sighed. 'Sorry, guys. I know I need to decide, but it's so hard.'

'Well, I hate to sound like your parents, but we'll support you too,' Hannah said. 'It would be horrible if you missed the show, but maybe we'll get another chance to perform it.'

'Maybe,' I said, but I knew it wouldn't be the same.

One way or the other, I was going to have to choose.

Chapter Twenty-six

The big day was finally here. I took my time getting dressed, knowing that soon I'd be the focus of so many people's attention. I'd spent a lot of time planning this outfit, and I wanted everything to be just perfect. I examined myself in the mirror. Yes, I decided, I would do.

Sadie tapped on the door. 'Are you ready, darling?'

'Yes, come in,' I called. I turned around so Sadie could get a clear view.

'Oh, Meg, you look amazing!' she told me. 'Now all you need is a little bit of make-up. I know you're only twelve but this is a special occasion after all. Let me see what I have.'

When she had finished Sadie stood back to admire her work. 'Fabulous, darling! Let me take a photo, and then we'd better get going.'

In the car, Sadie kept up a steady patter, commenting on everything we passed by. I replied in monosyllables, too nervous to focus on what she was saying. This was it!

Sadie parked just outside the hall. I got out of the car, my beads clacking together, and untangled my purple feather boa which had got caught in the seatbelt.

'Meg, you're here!' Hannah came running up to me, squealing in excitement. She looked fantastic in her outfit, and she had put on thick orange foundation just like mine, and bright green eyeshadow. Laura and Ruby weren't far behind, dressed in their costumes too and looking completely hyper.

'Well of course,' I said, smiling around at my friends. 'I wouldn't miss this for the world!'

'I love your beauty spot!' Hannah said, admiring the spot Sadie had drawn near my top lip. 'You really look the part!'

'So do you,' I told her. 'Everyone does. I'm so excited!'

'Me too!' Hannah and Laura said.

'I'm terrified!' Ruby said.

'Me too,' the rest of us admitted, laughing.

'Well, ladies, we'd better go in, your audience will be here soon, and you can't be seen in costume!' Sadie said. 'I believe there's going to be quite a turn-out today.'

'Where's your grandad?' Ruby asked as we made our way into the school.

'He's keeping guard at the front of the hall,' I told her. 'Making sure we don't have any, um, unwanted guests.'

'Brilliant!' Ruby said.

Miss Brennan came rushing up to us as we entered the

classroom near the hall which was going to be the 'back stage' area.

'Oh good, you're here!' she said. 'You look wonderful, all of you! Now, you know how the programme works, don't you? We have the fifth class singing first – then their drama piece – then sixth class singing – and your drama piece is the last act.'

We all nodded, though Hannah whispered to me, 'I wish we weren't last! It's so nerve-wracking!'

I didn't mind, though. This for me was almost the best part – the anticipation of going on stage, knowing the audience was out there waiting for us to transform into our characters.

Sadie's mobile rang. 'Meg, it's your mum,' she told me.

I took the phone into a quiet corner of the classroom.

'Meg, darling – all set for your performance? Sadie sent me a photo – you look amazing!'

'Thanks, Mum,' I said. 'How was the premiere?'

'Wonderful!' Mum said. 'All glittery frocks and flashing lights and razzmatazz. We've just been to an after-show party and we're going on to another one. I'd forgotten how much I enjoy it all, darling. I'm so sorry to miss your performance, but Grandad has promised to record the whole thing for me.'

'I think he's a bit busy at the moment,' I said with a grin, 'but I'm sure he'll be ready in time for the start of our piece.

I'd better go, Mum. Miss Brennan wants us in our places.'

'Good luck!'

I peeped into the hall. Even though I'd known there was quite a crowd coming, it was still a shock to see it so full. There must have been hundreds of parents, past pupils and local people, with the Lord Mayor in the best seat, sitting beside the principal. In front of the seated rows the younger classes sat on the floor, ready to watch the show.

Behind the closed stage curtains, fifth class were already in their places on the stage, lined up in neat rows in their school uniforms. They were whispering and giggling together, despite the best efforts of their teacher to shush them.

Just then, Isabel arrived, her face a picture. 'Meg, your grandad is amazing!' she told me, giggling.

'What did he do?' I asked, hardly daring to hope it had all been sorted out already.

'There was some reporter at the school door, trying to get in to see the show,' Isabel told us breathlessly. 'Your grandad just took her by the elbow and walked her right off the school property, telling her it was invited guests only. She started protesting that she was an aunt of a pupil in the school but he told her it was a media-free zone. Then he said she was trespassing and if she didn't leave at once he was going to call the police.'

'Woohoo! Hurray for Meg's grandad!' Laura cried.

'Three cheers, everyone!'

'No thank you, Laura,' Miss Brennan said hastily. 'The show is about to start, we need to be quiet back here.'

I glowed with pride. Good old Grandad – I should have known I could trust him not to let anyone ruin our day.

Behind us, Tracey had a face like thunder. I smiled to myself. All her scheming had come to nothing.

The time sped by all too quickly, and soon sixth class were finishing their last song and it was time for us to go up on stage. The stage curtains were drawn and our class-mates began to leave the stage, going in to the hall where they could watch the rest of the show.

'I hope you fall off the stage and break your leg,' Tracey hissed at me as she went by.

'Thank you, Tracey,' I said. 'That's so kind.' Seeing her confused look, I added, 'Didn't you know that "break a leg" is how theatre people wish each other luck?'

Not waiting for an answer, I stepped up onto the stage, clutching Hannah's hand in excitement. I thought of Mum and Dad at their after-show party dressed in their fancy clothes. And I thought of Sadie and Grandad, out there in the school hall, waiting to watch me perform. Some day, a long way off, maybe I'd be happy to be Daisy Sheri-dan, going to premieres and being chased by paparazzi. But right now, it was enough of a thrill just being me.